Lone Eagle

Lone Eagle

A Novel

by
Alfred Dennis

iUniverse, Inc.
New York Bloomington Shanghai

Lone Eagle

Copyright © 2008 by Alfred M. Dennis

All rights reserved. No part of this book may be used or reproduced by any means, graphic, electronic, or mechanical, including photocopying, recording, taping or by any information storage retrieval system without the written permission of the publisher except in the case of brief quotations embodied in critical articles and reviews.

iUniverse books may be ordered through booksellers or by contacting:

iUniverse
1663 Liberty Drive
Bloomington, IN 47403
www.iuniverse.com
1-800-Authors (1-800-288-4677)

Because of the dynamic nature of the Internet, any Web addresses or links contained in this book may have changed since publication and may no longer be valid.

This is a work of fiction. All of the characters, names, incidents, places, organizations, and dialogue in this novel are either the products of the author's imagination or are used fictitiously.

ISBN: 978-0-595-49145-2 (pbk)
ISBN: 978-0-595-60983-3 (ebk)

Printed in the United States of America

Acknowledgements

I would like to thank my great friends for their help on Lone Eagle.
Jerry Nelson, Doris McIntosh, Ida Byrd and my sister Betty Solomon.

1

The horse labored with every stride, his nostrils flared wide, bringing in every breath of lifesaving air his tired body could consume. The lathered horse had run several miles over rough, hard ground that tore at his unshod hooves. Still, the great animal surged forward, his powerful legs keeping the man on his back safe from the oncoming enemy behind. The big gelding was blowing hard, too hard; concern showed in the blue eyes of the rider when he turned to look at the warriors that followed.

Only the great heart of the animal had kept him alive this far, but the horse wasn't going much farther, refuge had to be found, and soon. Fighting the many warriors that followed would be suicide. Armed only with a cap and ball pistol, and hunting knife, he wouldn't be able to put up much of a fight.

The little mustangs that carried the oncoming warriors were small but tough as iron. The larger gelding was faster, but when he slowed to save energy and rest, the warriors closed the gap between them.

The man's blue eyes searched ahead desperately; time was running out with every faltering stride of the great animal. Turning again in the saddle he took in the streaked faces of his pursuers. The distance was too great to make eye contact, but there was no mistaking the hideous war cries or the brandishing bows. He must find something soon. Turning again to the front, the man touched the riding whip hanging from his saddle, then with a smile he dropped the whip and ran his hand gently along the sweat stained neck of the struggling gelding.

"No old son, you've done your best; now it's up to me to run the rest of this race."

The war cries were getting louder; he knew without looking back his pursuers were closing the gap. The gelding had no more run left in him; the warriors could see him faltering, and yelled in anticipation of the upcoming kill.

Passing through a shallow belt of timber, the man grinned, and let out his own yell of defiance that carried back to the onrushing warriors, making them curious of what the white man had to yell about. On a raid to the east they were unfamiliar with this country, and unaware of the great river ahead.

Thirty yards from the river the gelding stumbled sending the rider far over his head. Rolling quickly to his feet, the man looked at the wind broke horse, then sprinted towards the river and safety. Shedding his heavy woolen uniform top with the Lieutenants bars, the man dove far out into the swift current. Bobbing to the top the man looked to where the warriors were emerging from the timber. Diving again before he was spotted, the man swam as far underwater as his lungs would permit before resurfacing.

"There," a brown arm shot out, pinpointing the blond head of hair far out in the river. Several arrows flew harmlessly past the swimming man.

"He's mine," a slender built warrior exclaimed as he whipped his horse into the murky water, then bailed off stroking powerfully towards the fleeing white.

Looking back the man was relieved he was out of effective arrow range, but was shocked when he saw the dark face coming towards him, a large skinning knife clutched between his teeth. Slowing his strokes the white man knew he couldn't outswim the oncoming warrior. He would have to conserve his strength for the deadly battle ahead. The warriors on the bank yelled their encouragement as their comrade closed the distance between himself and his quarry.

"Aye, the Wolverine is a strong swimmer," A large warrior grinned, his eyes riveted on the drama unfolding out in the river.

"Yes, my Chief, no one in the Pawnee village is stronger," another put in.

"The white eye tires; he is slowing."

"The Wolverine will have his glory this day."

A few feet separated the two swimmers when both men disappeared beneath the murky waters. A slender brown arm, wielding a knife that flashed in the sunlight, raised above the water line then disappeared. Again and again the knife flashed; then a great swell came from the water as both men surfaced locked together in mortal combat. The warriors yelled encouragement, and then became quiet as the two men sank out of sight.

Again they surfaced; this time a white arm, heavily muscled, was wrapped around the throat of the warrior. Slowly the two men sank out of sight. A sudden heave of the water and the blond hair reappeared and yelled defiantly at the warriors on the bank.

Stroking slowly towards the far shore the white man was shocked when he heard the crack of a rifle go off in front of him.

"Keep a stroking sonny, we'uns got that bunch of red heathens on the run." A buckskin clad arm shot out and pulled him bodily from the current of the mighty Missouri River.

Collapsing on the river's edge the lieutenant pulled great volumes of air into his lungs. The huge mountain man laughed, then patted him on the back.

"You'll do soldier, yes siree bob, you'll do." The one that seemed like the leader nodded his head approvingly.

The blond headed man looked up at the hunters and nodded his head. "I don't want to seem discourteous but I'm in a great hurry to get to Philadelphia; it's very urgent."

"How can we help?"

"I need to buy a horse from you."

"We won't sell you one soldier, but for that show you just put on, you walk right over there and take whichever one that suits you." The leader pointed to where several horses stood ground tied. "And you're welcome."

"Well if I can ever repay you in anyway, my name's Preston Forbes and I thank you." The tall lieutenant mounted a rangy bay gelding and waved as he turned towards the east and kicked the horse into a hard lope.

2

The Lieutenant stepped tiredly down from the two horse hack that had brought him from Philadelphia to the suburbs. Before him stood Lane Manor, the stately home of General Horatio Lane and his two grandchildren, William and Virginia.

William was his best friend; and Virginia, ah Virginia, the prettiest woman, well girl in all Philadelphia. A warm smile spread across the rugged countenance of the tall man, as he remembered the beautiful little red head as he had last seen her. Two years had passed since his graduation from West Point Military Academy and his assignment to Fort Laramie in the west.

Looking down at the stained buckskin shirt the trappers had given him when they fished him from the Missouri River he was almost too ashamed to knock on the heavy oak door before him. A heavy robust woman dressed in the black and white attire of a servant answered and stepped back in surprise.

"Why, Master Forbes!"

"Millie, how are you?"

"Just fine, Sir."

"Millie, who is it?" A woman's voice asked from the interior of the house. The man's finger went to his lips in a signal for the maid not to answer.

"Millie," The woman appeared and was about to ask again when she saw the tall figure before her. "Press," she whispered, and for a moment the man thought she was going to faint.

"Virginia?" The name was more of a question as the man stepped forward and stared unbelieving at the woman before him.

"Press, what are? Oh, my hair." The young woman stammered running her hand over her bright red hair, then straightening her dress. "Excuse me, Preston Forbes, but you could have had the courtesy to warn a lady you were coming."

She fumed in mock anger, then threw herself into his arms. "What are you doing here? Your last letter said you were in Montana Territory or some heathen place like that."

"Well, Miss Gin, if you will quiet down I will tell you what I'm doing here." He smiled down into her green eyes.

"Okay, put me down and I'll be quiet."

"Promise?"

"I promise,"

"There." He lowered her to the floor never taking his eyes from the lovely face, a face even more beautiful than he remembered.

"Well?"

"Well, first tell me where Bill and the General are."

"They sir, are in the library discussing business. Business much too dull for a lady's ear; at least, that's their excuse for keeping me out." She faked pouting, causing her mouth to turn up at the corners.

"What lady?"

"Why you!" She pretended to slap him, and then stepped into his arms again."Oh Press, I've missed you; it's good to have you home."

"Enough that I've earned a kiss?"

"Why Mister Forbes, a lady doesn't kiss a gentleman in her foyer in broad daylight.

"Who's a gentleman?" he answered pulling her small frame to his.

"What's the meaning of this, Sir?"

Setting the woman down Press turned to where two men, both tall and stately stood smiling at them. In one gigantic stride the younger of the two embraced Press in a bear hug that would have crushed an oak tree. Grinning at each other the two friends wrestled around in circles before they stopped in front of the older man.

"Preston my boy, it's good to have you home." The older man extended his hand.

"General Lane," Press grasped the extended hand of the older man, a hand still strong even though the General had to be in his late sixties.

"Into the library with you Sir, you're probably in need of something to wash down the dust you've gathered on your trip." The General motioned towards the door behind them.

"I could indeed, but a bath and some clean clothes that don't smell are probably more appropriate before I am suitable for a lady's company." Press winked at Virginia.

"Since when is Gin a lady?" Bill chimed in. "The last time you two were together, as I recall, you sir wound up in a horse trough."

"My granddaughter is a lady and a beautiful one at that." The General smiled adoringly at Virginia.

"Yes Sir, she is." Press agreed staring at Virginia.

"No bath old friend, until you have told us how and why you are here. By the looks of you it was a hard journey." Bill propelled Press towards the open door.

Entering, Press let his eyes wander over the familiar room, a beautiful room, filled with plush rugs and magnificent paintings, a room that had always fascinated him. A portrait of Andy Jackson hung over the fireplace, the blazing personality as hot as the fire itself.

The General passed Press and Bill filled wine glasses and was about to propose a toast, but was stopped by the sound of Virginia clearing her throat.

"What about mine, Grandfather?"

"You're a little young, lass." The old man smiled.

"Yes my dear sister and still too young to entertain men in the foyer." Bill quipped.

"That's what you know, sweet brother." She laughed, winking at Press.

Clearing his throat, General Lane instantly quieted the two siblings, then turned to where Press had sat down heavily on the settee. "Preston my boy, I can see you're tired from your long journey. We will talk after you rest and clean up."

Press agreed he was tired. In the last four weeks he had crossed nearly fifteen hundred miles through hostile country, and hostile natives, as fast as horse flesh could carry him. Now that he was here facing the three people he cared for most in the world, he wasn't so sure he should divulge the information he carried. Nothing could bring him to hurt these three people, but should he withhold something as important as a brother? Studying the faces in front of him he knew what the answer would be.

"I thank you Sir, perhaps it would be better if the news I carry waited until I am rested."

"Virginia, would you show Preston to his room?" The General asked, knowing full well that after seven years in this house Press could find his own way. The wise old warrior wanted the two youngsters to have a moment alone.

"Till supper then." Press bowed to Bill and the General, then followed Virginia from the room.

"You know I'm curious?" Virginia turned as the door closed.

"You, my dear, are always curious."

"But what's so important to bring you home and ... She quieted looking him up and down.

"And what?"

"Disheveled, I've never seen you with three weeks beard and dirty clothes on before."

"Is it that bad?"

"No, quite to the contrary, my dear sir, it gives you character."

"Is that good?"

"Oh yes." She answered, standing on her tip toes to give him a quick kiss.

"Maybe, I should only bathe on Friday nights?"

"As long as you're here I wouldn't care."

"I'll bet, you'd probably put me into the horse trough again." Press grinned, remembering the time she had accidently knocked him into the wooden trough.

"That was an accident and you know it was."

"Well, anyway you did apologize." Press smiled remembering their first kiss.

Blushing, Virginia retreated from the room. Smiling, Press watched her retreat down the stairs, then entered his room to find Millie had already poured his bath water and laid out some clean clothes for him. Making a mental note to thank her he stripped his soiled clothes from his lean frame and lowered himself into the hot water.

3

It seemed to Press that he had just closed his eyes when the door opened and Bill started rousing him awake.

"Supper time Lieutenant Forbes."

"Already?"

"Already, you've been sleeping nearly ten hours. Virginia had Millie hold dinner two hours. Now fall out soldier, I'm hungry."

"Yes Sir," Press answered so tired he didn't remember getting out of the tub and into bed.

Dinner was always formal at Lane Manor so Press dressed in a dark coat, dress pants and a silk shirt, remnants of his pre West Point days. Bill waited patiently, his huge frame wrapped around a straight chair, watching his friend shave and comb his thick blond hair.

"It must be really important?"

Turning, Press grinned. "You know you and Gin are about the most curious two people I've ever met."

"All right, all right, pretend I didn't ask." Bill pouted, pretending hurt feelings.

"That won't work either."

"And I thought we were friends."

"And I thought you were hungry."

"Starved."

"Let's eat, then my friend you'll find out." Then in a more serious mood Press added. "I hope you're going to like what I have to say."

"Me too, old friend, and by the way I've got a surprise downstairs for you, too."

"What?"

"You wouldn't be the curious kind too, now would you?"

Press just grinned. Coming downstairs the two friends heard laughter coming from the library. Entering first, Press found the General and Virginia deep in conversation with a tall raven haired woman about the same age as Virginia.

"My darling." Bill leaned down and kissed the woman on the cheek. "Preston Forbes, may I present my fiancée Miss Elizabeth Hudson."

Press bowed slightly. "I am honored, madam."

"Sir, Bill has told me so much about you."

"Nothing bad, I hope?"

"Rest assured Sir, Bill would soundly thrash anyone speaking ill of you."

"Have you known Bill long?" Press was curious, Bill had never shown enough interest in any one girl long enough to become engaged.

"Since I went to work for General Lane."

"Two years now, I believe." Bill chimed in, beaming with pride.

"Exactly one year, eleven months, and twenty three days." The woman corrected Bill.

"What no hours?" Press grinned.

"Miss Hudson is our bookkeeper," the General answered. "And I might add the best we've ever had. We're lucky to have obtained her services, and I am very pleased she is to be in my family soon."

Bill started to say something but was interrupted as Millie came in announcing dinner was served. Press turned to where Virginia sat, taking in her beautiful evening gown, a blue dress that accented her red hair and green eyes, making her even more elegant.

"May I?" Press offered his arm to Virginia.

The dining hall was as extravagant as everything else in Lane Manor. General Horatio Lane was considered rich even in conservative circles, wealth coming from commerce and trade, two enterprises at which he was exceptional. His trading companies extended from Boston to Richmond and across the waters to Europe. Yes, the General was a very wealthy man, but his greatest assets were his good name and honesty.

Serving with Andy Jackson from Horseshoe Bend to New Orleans, and being a close friend and confidante, he had been offered, but refused, a post in Jackson's new government. He had built his own empire, and it showed in abundance in this exquisite dining room.

Dinner finished, everyone retired to the library where the General poured wine. Bill laid another log on the fire to stave off the chill in the room. Springtime was coming but the nights still turned cold quickly.

"Now everyone." The General raised his glass towards Press. "A toast, a toast to Preston whom I consider as my own."

"To Press." Everyone, including Virginia, whom the General had surprised by pouring her a drink, raised their glasses.

"To Preston, and his safe return to us."

Everyone chimed in their agreement and touched glasses. Press grinned as Virginia coughed, but he was wise enough to hold back the chuckle that was building in his chest. Not so with Bill who had to have a little fun with his sister.

"I told you, Grandfather, about letting little children drink."

Press handed Virginia a glass of water which she accepted gratefully. "Careful Sis, that water has a real bite to it." Bill just naturally had to rib her, but no brother was as protective or caring as Bill.

Bill had always noticed the difference in Virginia from other girls. Her small frame held a strong inner strength and a calmness that always astounded him. Even as a small child she was so sure of herself, so confident in everything she did. Noticing Press staring at Virginia, Bill knew his friend felt the same.

"Now ladies and gentlemen, I believe Preston has come a long ways to give us some important information." The General turned the floor over to Press and seated himself.

Well here it is, Press thought to himself as he faced the four expectant faces. Setting his glass down he studied each face, wondering how they were going to take his news. Looking at Virginia last, he was relieved at the quick wink of encouragement she gave him.

"Well, to start with, as you all are aware, I have just returned from the Northwest Territories of Nebraska and the Dakotas. Some of what I'm about to tell you, you already know. So, if you will bear with me for a few minutes I will fill Miss Hudson in on a little family history. I'm sure Bill has told you he was a twin. A brother was lost somewhere in Colorado Territory in the early thirties when they were about three years of age. I myself became familiar with the Lane story after Bill and I became acquainted in a back alley in Philadelphia, where some thugs were trying to rearrange his ugly face." Press grinned.

"My William is certainly not ugly, Sir." Virginia chided Press good naturedly.

"Anyway, after our graduation from West Point Military Academy, again thanks to General Lane for getting me appointed, I chose a military career while Bill decided to return to the family trading business. Immediately, I was assigned to the west where I was assigned to Colonel Dobbs dragoons at Fort Laramie. In my capacity as post adjutant I was present at all councils and treaties between the tribes and our government. It was at the treaty of forty nine that I saw a young warrior, a sub chief, a man so greatly thought of by his people that he is, in spite of his young years, held in high esteem, and his words carry considerable weight in their councils.

The council was in its second day when this warrior stepped into the council circle causing every warrior there to immediately become quiet, so quiet you could hear babies crying in the village half a mile away.

I have never seen a better physical specimen, at least three inches over six feet, heavily muscled, not an ounce of fat on him. I had by now picked up a fair amount of the local dialect from the hangers on at the fort, and a little sign language.

"What's sign language?" Virginia inquired intrigued.

"Talking with their hands, like this." Press motioned a few signs for her.

"From what I could make out, this young chief was bitterly haranguing the older chiefs, and cussing whites for every despicable thing he could think of."

"Why whites?" Bill asked.

"Whites have caused considerable suffering to the tribes, disease, whiskey drinking, and cheating them out of their furs."

"Press, what is all this leading up to?" Bill questioned again.

"Just this," Press hesitated. "And I hope you understand why I bring this news. I firmly believe this young warrior who they call Lone Eagle could be Phillip."

"Preposterous!" Bill exclaimed jumping to his feet.

"Why preposterous Sir?"

"Phillip was killed along with our father and mother in Colorado Territory when their wagon train was wiped out."

"His body was never found; yet, you and Virginia survived."

"Virginia and William survived because they were under an overturned wagon and weren't discovered until the next day by a passing army patrol." The General put in calmly.

"Sir, I believe this Lone Eagle and Phillip are one and the same." Press continued.

"Why do you believe this?" Bill asked again perplexed.

"For one thing, Sioux raiders have been all the way to Mexico on raids. It is a known fact that they bring back their young male captives to raise as their own, and lastly, you and this warrior are as much alike as two peas in a pod."

"Did you talk with this Lone Eagle?" Virginia asked, excitement rising in her voice.

"No."

"And why not if you thought he was Phillip? For pete's sake Press, if this is the news you have rode so far to bring, I think you've taken leave of your senses." Bill retorted hotly.

"If that's the way you feel old friend, I'll not say more. I'll be heading back in the morning."

"No." Virginia spoke sharply. Everyone turned to where she sat, her hands clasped together tightly. "What's the matter with you Bill? Press has ridden all the way here and you treat him like a complete stranger, or worse. Go ahead Press, I for one want to hear more." She looked daggers at Bill, daring him to say more.

Shrugging, Bill turned to the fire; his face beet red from the dressing down Virginia had given him in front of Elizabeth.

"This is a painful subject for all of you, and especially Grandfather Lane, so I will leave it up to him." Press looked at the old General who was deep in thought.

For several minutes the General looked into the fire, his face a mask. Finally, clearing his throat, he looked to where Press stood.

"Preston my son, no man alive has more respect for your judgment than I. What you say is true. This is a very painful subject for me as both my son and his wife are dead, and now you say Phillip may be alive. But, I agree with Virginia, we will hear you out on this matter."

"Very well Sir, as I was saying, I do believe this young warrior to be Phillip; the likeness is uncanny. Put Bill in long hair and a breechcloth and I could not tell them apart."

"Come now, Press." Bill interrupted again.

"Don't you think as dark as you are that if you were dressed like an Indian and out in the elements all the time you'd look like one?"

"Maybe; perish the thought."

"One of the old mountain men knew a little about the story of this Lone Eagle. His courage in battle is already legendary. His father is named Tall Bow, a much honored warrior of the Ogallalla Sioux. This old trapper says legend has it that a boy child was delivered to Tall Bow by the great spirits. In plain words this probably means the boy was not of Tall Bow's loins but taken on a raid and adopted by the warrior."

"If this is so how would we go about finding out the truth?" The General chimed in, beginning to get excited.

"Now Grandfather, don't go get your hopes up too much." Bill warned.

"By your attitude, big brother, it appears you don't want to find Phillip." Virginia frowned at Bill.

"To the contrary, but this is so farfetched." Bill retorted.

"It may be, but I don't think so." Press turned to Bill.

"My apologies old friend, you know that I trust your judgment completely, but it has been so many years."

"Yes it has, a lot of years. But, I would stake my reputation that this is Phillip."

"They do say that everyone has an identical twin somewhere." Elizabeth put in, trying to ease Bill's position on the matter.

"That's true Miss Hudson, but there is one more thing."

"And what would that be?" Bill asked.

"You told me your grandfather could only tell you two apart by a scar over Phillip's left eye; a scar you said he received from a fall."

"This man has a scar?" the General asked hoarsely.

"Yes, over his left eye."

"Sir, would you indulge an old man and tell me of this scar?"

"Certainly, but it would be better if I draw it for you, but I'm not much of an artist."

"The best you can do will be fine."

Press took the pencil and paper from the outstretched hand of the elder Lane and quickly sketched a picture, then two more before he was satisfied. Handing the paper to the General he heard the old warrior's excited exclamation.

Everyone started firing questions at Press at the same time. It was well past midnight when Bill excused himself and Elizabeth, leaving him alone with Virginia. General Lane had already retired for the evening.

"How are we going to find out the truth?" Virginia leaned back against Press on the settee.

"I don't know."

"If we could get him to come here."

"Getting him to come here would be impossible."

"Then how?"

"Probably with plenty of trade goods and a good interpreter, a man we could trust completely."

"You said you knew their language."

"Some, enough to get by, but not enough to handle this delicate a situation."

"Why is it so delicate to ask a man about his family?"

"These people are wild; you have to understand their religion, how they think, their taboos."

"Is he really that wild?"

Press nodded. "I've never seen a more fierce and imposing man in my life."

"If he is Phillip, he is a good man."

"I didn't say he was a bad man, I said he was wild and fierce, as wild as any animal. You corner him and he becomes deadly."

"Not Phillip."

"If this goes any farther, I hope you're right young lady."
"Surely we must find a way."
"That'll be up to the General."
"I know Grandfather, he'll find a way."
"Yes, you're probably right. Now young lady it's past your bedtime."
"Not yet."
"Tomorrow might be a big day."
"I don't want this moment to end." She snuggled closer.

Looking down into her beautiful eyes he brushed a stray lock of hair from her brow. "You are beautiful."
"Am I?"
"Very."
"It seemed you were gone forever."
"Forever is a long time."
"Did you think often of me?"
"Never a day or hour passed that I didn't think of you."
"Why?"
"I don't know, maybe I didn't have anyone to throw in the water trough." Press grinned.

"You, ooh!" Leaping to her feet, Virginia clenched her fists, stomping from the room leaving Press behind to wonder at her quick outburst. Rushing from the room Virginia almost ran over Millie.

"Women." Press muttered out loud.
"What's wrong with women, Master Forbes?"
"I'll never understand them, that's what's wrong."
"No, men never do, but I hope you're smart enough to understand love." Millie turned from the room.
"Love? Who's talking about love?"
"You can't see? Then you must be blind too." Millie shook her head at Press and left the room.

4

The next morning Press arrived for breakfast refreshed and eager to see Virginia. Millie's parting words the previous evening still sounded in his ears, causing a warm feeling in his chest.

"Good morning, Sir," Press greeted the General who was already seated at the dining table.

"Preston, my boy, and how was your sleep?"

"Fine, slept like a baby."

"Yes, I wish it were so with these old bones, but I'm glad you slept well because we have much to do today."

"We do?" Press was dejected at the news as he wanted to spend the day with Virginia.

The General leaned towards Press and laid down his napkin. "My boy, it's very difficult for me to believe you have found Phillip; however, I've got to know one way or the other if it is indeed my grandson."

"Yes sir,"

"Now, tell me what we need to do."

Press studied the stern face of a General in front of him, not the face of a grandfather. He knew this was more of an order than a request. Going into great detail, he described the difficult journey ahead, and the many things that would be needed.

"I want you to make out a list of supplies, armaments, and trade goods that you have mentioned. I will be leaving for Philadelphia this morning to outfit this army."

"Army, Sir?"

"I will arrange for an indefinite leave of absence for you, providing of course, that you will agree to lead us?"

"Us, Sir? Will you be going General?"

"Certainly."

Press sat his coffee down. "But Grandfather Lane, this is a long and perilous journey."

"I will be going, and so will Virginia, Bill and probably Elizabeth."

"The girls?" Press was shocked. He hadn't planned on the General going, much less the women. He was undecided whether he was delighted or worried. "Begging your pardon, General, any place west of St. Louis is no place for two young ladies and a sixty five year old man." Press quickly added Sir again. He knew the General's temper and wanted to avoid any part of it.

"To the contrary, Sir, I think it's just the place for us."

"But General."

"Lieutenant Forbes, may I remind you Sir, you are addressing a Major General of the United States Army and my orders will be obeyed. We are all going."

"Yes Sir." Press knew the old General was serious.

"If this is Phillip, I will see all of my grandchildren together again before I'm gone."

"Sir, you will outlive us all."

"Maybe, maybe not, but we're all going west."

"What's all this talk of going somewhere?" Bill questioned, walking into the kitchen.

"You tell him Preston, I'm on my way to Philadelphia. And I'll expect you two to get things started while I'm gone."

"Started?" Bill looked questioningly at Press. "Started where?"

"West." Press studied the General's back as he left the room.

Bill groaned, setting down heavily, making the wooden chair moan under his great weight. "I knew it."

"What do you think?"

"I think, old buddy, you should have confided in me first. Now you've done it."

"Maybe, but would you have told him?"

"I don't know."

"It's his right."

"He's getting old; it could kill him."

"It could, but he may just find his missing grandson."

"You may be right; anyway there's no sense crying over spilt milk, and I'm hungry."

"You're always hungry," Virginia said entering the dining room and purposely ignoring Press.

"I'm a growing boy."

"Good morning, Gin." Press grinned at the little red head.

"Sir."

"Sir, is that all you can say?"

"Well, let me see now, I suppose I could say good morning Sir, how about throwing me in the water trough."

"Uh oh." Bill grinned. "You two are getting an early start."

"Both of you had better eat and get to work like Grandfather told you."

"How do you know what he told us?" Press asked.

"She knows everything." Bill quipped, downing a hot biscuit.

"Where's Elizabeth?"

"She's in the kitchen washing dishes."

"What happened to Millie?" Bill turned to where Elizabeth had appeared at the kitchen door.

"She went to Philadelphia with the General." Elizabeth placed a platter of flapjacks in front of the men.

"What for?" Bill was curious.

"I'll tell you what for; we've been had." Press nodded at Bill.

"And what exactly does that mean?"

"It means while we slept, these two convinced the General to take them along with us."

"West?" Bill almost choked on his breakfast.

"Well those Indians sure aren't east of us."

"We'll see about that." Bill bellowed, rising from his chair.

"You're right Bill, I should have told you first."

"Don't worry Mister Forbes," Virginia smirked. "We won't slow you down, but just in case, why don't you carry the water trough, and if we do you can drown us."

"You know," Press said rising from his chair, "that water trough might not be such a bad idea right now."

"You wouldn't dare, Sir. Grandfather would have your hide."

"Grandfather isn't here is he?" Press said tossing Virginia over his shoulder, surprised at how light she was.

"Preston Forbes, you put me down right now."

Press was about to reply, but Elizabeth joined the battle, pouring a whole tin of red pepper down Press's shirt, causing him to drop Virginia and grab his nose. Threatening Bill with a tin of molasses, they ran both men from the house.

"Try the water trough Mister Forbes, it'll take the edge off your pepper." The girls laughed, watching the two men retreat towards the barn.

"It's a long way to the Dakota's girls." Bill retorted, propelling Press towards the water trough.

"I thought you were in love with him?" Elizabeth questioned as they watched Press strip his shirt off.

"Oh, he doesn't know it yet, but he's going to marry me. Look at the muscles, Liz." Virginia was watching the muscles flex in Press' arms and chest as he washed.

"Virginia Lane, you get in here right now." Elizabeth propelled the little red head inside. "You are supposed to be a lady."

"Well, don't ladies like muscles?"

"Virginia, I swear." Elizabeth shook her head.

"Well, don't they?"

5

A full week of hard work and long days passed before everything was packed and ready. Bill had purchased a new Conestoga wagon and four heavy bay draft horses. The General had made arrangements for his nephew, Jeremy Lane, to take charge of all Lane Enterprises in his absence for however long he was needed.

The girls, despite considerable arguing, were allowed only the dire essentials for the trip, causing them to blame the pepper incident on Press not allowing them to take along their entire wardrobe of dresses. Press had supplied the wagon with enough supplies to see them through to St. Louis, where he intended to re-supply.

Lastly, plenty of powder and shot had been loaded for the Hawkins Rifles the General had provided from his game room. The wagon carried a good supply of pistols and knives, plenty for trade purposes down the trail.

"Well, I think we have everything that's on your list." Press thought the General looked out of place in rough denim as he peered inside the wagon. Only enough room was left for the girls to sleep at night, or in rough weather.

"We're as ready as we'll ever be." Press agreed.

"Good, I propose we all take the rest of the day off and prepare for the girl's party."

Virginia and Elizabeth had planned a going away party for their last night, arguing with the General that it would be inexcusable to leave without saying farewell to all of their friends and having one more chance to wear their beautiful evening gowns. By six o'clock several carriages had arrived carrying their guests, most of whom were the young and wealthy of Philadelphia's elite. Seeing the young men arrive in their best suits Bill commented to Press that maybe it wasn't such a bad idea to take the girls instead of leaving them unprotected around these wolves.

The band had struck up a lively tune by the time Press had dressed and come downstairs. Entering the grand ballroom, he found Virginia dancing gracefully in the arms of Theodore Rush, one of Press's most disliked acquaintances. Many a day they had exchanged black eyes and bloody noses in school.

"Aha, good old Theodore again I see." Bill quipped arriving at his friend's side.

"Who else?" Press replied, gaining control of his temper. "Let's have a go at the punch bowl."

"I've got the ingredients; ah Press, no trouble or the General will have your hide hung out. You know how he feels about guests in his home."

"I know."

Laughing, they sauntered towards the large punch bowl the girls had prepared. Knowing how mad it made Virginia, Bill always was willing to spike the bowl a little; none of the guest ever complained.

"There." Bill grinned emptying the bottle into the punch.

"A little much, wasn't it?"

"What the heck, it's our last night."

"When Virginia tastes that stuff it may be your last night, period." Press laughed out loud.

Press danced with several different ladies but none with Virginia as she seemed to be taken with old Theodore. When the band took a break, he stepped out on the veranda to cool his flaring temper.

"It's a beautiful night, isn't it?"

Turning at the sound of Virginia's voice, Press expected to find her with Theodore. "What?"

"The moon shining over the river." She replied stepping closer.

"Yes."

"Press, it's our last party for who knows how long, lets have a good time."

"Truce." He smiled down at her. "You know fighting with you isn't fun anymore."

Moving closer to him she raised her beautiful face to his. "Maybe you don't like me anymore?"

"No, I think we've finally grown up." He answered pulling her into his arms.

"Well, well, what do we have here, love birds?"

Separating, Virginia and Press turned to find Theodore smiling wickedly at them. "I followed you outside, my dear to see if you needed company, but I see you are in good hands already."

A crushing right hand sent Theodore through the banister, landing him in the shrubbery. Sounds of the crashing wood brought several guests outside, just in time to see Press knock Theodore senseless.

Bill stepped forward and grabbed Press, pulling him from the prone body of Theodore. "I think he's had enough."

Letting the tenseness go out of his body, Press looked down at the unconscious man. Dragging Theodore to the water trough he dumped the limp man into the frigid water.

Returning to where Virginia stood he extended his arm. "May I have this dance, Miss Lane?"

"This one, Sir, and all the rest to come."

6

Nine weeks and one thousand miles had passed since the tearful farewell with Millie and Lane Manor. Virginia had watched as the large mansion, the only home she had ever known, faded slowly from sight.

The General and Virginia had taken turns driving, but today he had insisted on doing all the driving, anxiously watching for the first signs of Independence to come into view. Virginia had retreated to the tailgate of the wagon where she could talk quietly with Press.

Riding slowly, the Hawkins resting over the pommel of his saddle, the tall man smiled and chatted with the little red head. The flowers were in full bloom as there had been plenty of rain, and the grass was lush and green. The air smelled sweetly, with the odor of fresh honeysuckle. Only the squeaking and moaning of the wagon and plodding of the horses, interrupted the splendor of the day.

"Are we almost there?"

"Just a couple hours, I believe."

"Grandfather's anxious."

"I know."

"The sun feels good." She leaned back against the rough boards of the wagon.

Studying the clouds above them Press nodded. "It'll soon start getting hot."

"How much farther to Fort Laramie from Independence?"

"I'd guess about six or seven hundred miles."

"That far?"

"At least, are you getting tired of traveling?"

"A little, this wagon could jolt a pecan out of a squirrel's mouth."

Kicking the sorrel gelding alongside the wagon, Press slipped behind the saddle. "Come up here with me."

Grinning, Virginia stepped lightly into Press's outstretched arms. "Better?"

"Uh huh." She smiled, leaning back into his strong arms.

Independence came into view almost at sundown. As he pulled the team up in front of the first hotel he found, the General set the brake and climbed down, helping the girls down behind him. Unloading a clean change of clothes for everyone, Bill and Press set off for the stables, leaving the General to help the girls get rooms.

"Evening, Sir." Bill greeted the hostler as he stopped the wagon.

"Howdy gents."

"Do you have room for six horses?"

"Reckon so; that'll be six bits a day for grain and hay for each horse."

"That's fine." Bill climbed down from the wagon.

"Can't speak for the wagon or your belongings."

"How's that?"

"Lots of strangers in town."

"Don't worry mister; one of us will be with the wagon all the time." Bill assured the man.

The old hostler spit a stream of tobacco onto the hard packed earth. "Good, cause I ain't losing no sleep watching it."

Both young men grinned as the old man hobbled back towards the stable. Turning once to where Bill and Press were unharnessing the tired team, he shrugged then disappeared into the barn.

Propping the tongue of the wagon up, Press stretched the harness out on it up off the ground. Unsaddling the horses, Bill laid the saddles in the wagon out of the night dew, and put the wet blankets over the wagon wheels to dry. Brushing each horse in turn they checked for sores or galls.

"Well, I'll go eat right quick and come back and relieve you." Bill said, closing the corral gate behind the last horse.

Press nodded his agreement and pulled out a can of harness oil and a cloth and began to oil down the harness. "You got yourself a bad wore tug there pilgrim." Press hadn't heard the old hostler come up.

"Thank you, I'll see to it."

"Got an extra if'n you ain't."

"Thank you might have to take you up on that."
"Where you boys headed, if you don't mind saying?"
"Fort Laramie, Dakota Territory."
"Ya'll bible pumpers?"
"No sir?"
"Well you're not hunters, that's for sure."
"Why not?" Press grinned.
"Too prissy."
"We're looking for someone."
"Big country out there, good luck, you'll need it." The old hostler shook his head. "Goodnight then."
"A question for you sir."
"What'll that be?"
"Anyone you know getting up a wagon train heading west?"
"Might try down at McSweens in the morning."
"I'll do that, thank you."
"I'd be careful, if'n I were you."
"How come?"
"Like I said lots of tough fellers in town."
"Thanks, I'll remember."

Press returned to the harness, so deep in thought he did not hear Virginia and Bill walk up. "See, Sis, I told you he wouldn't miss you any."

"Here." Virginia took the oily rag from Press and handed it to Bill. "Oil your jaws as much as you talk, they need it."

Bill grinned as he watched Press and Virginia stroll slowly towards the hotel.

After a quick bath and change of clothes, Press rejoined Virginia in the dining hall. Seating themselves, Press ordered steak and potatoes and went to work on them as soon as they were served. The hall was decorated with buffalo heads, skulls, and deer racks. The room was rustic and rough, but the food was delicious.

Watching him eat, Virginia thought of what it would be like in their own home. Of course he was going to have to propose first. Feeling slightly guilty at her thoughts she smiled, no shame, just a woman who knows what she wants and goes after it.

"Penny for your thoughts?"

"Oh, nothing."

"Well, it must be my good looks," Press joked.

"My, aren't we conceited tonight?"

"Just tonight?"

"No you don't, not tonight. We're going to enjoy this evening, the last we may have for awhile."

"Yes, we need to move as quickly as possible."

"Because of the snows ahead?"

"Yes."

"Are they bad?"

"Well Gin, I'll tell you. One time I was camped, and during the night the snow around me melted. Well, when I woke up I was perched atop a tree almost a hundred feet in the air, horse and all. You should have seen that horse climbing down that tree. He was a might peeved at me."

"Press, I swear. You're beginning to lie as bad as Bill."

"You don't believe me?" Press pretended hurt feelings.

"Okay, I believe you, don't cry." She laughed, her beautiful smile bringing a smile from him in return.

"Children." the General motioned at the vacant chair. "May I?"

"Please do, maybe you can put a stop to some of Press' tall tales."

"Tall tales?"

"Never mind, I thought you were off to bed?"

"Presently my dear, I wanted a word with Preston first."

"Then I'll go see about Elizabeth."

"Sit, sit, Elizabeth is with Bill. Now my boy, how are we doing for time?"

"Fine Sir, providing of course we're not held up too long looking for a train to join."

"Let's hope not. I'll have us re-supplied first thing in the morning."

"Fine."

"Virginia and Elizabeth can help. I believe Virginia needed some more medicines and bandages for her medical bag."

"Medical bag?" Press asked curious.

"Why yes Press, I guess in the excitement I forgot to tell you I had been studying under Grandfather's good friend and former comrade at arms, Doctor Scott."

"A doctor, you're studying to be a doctor?"

"No, not quite. I don't think men are ready for a woman doctor yet. No, I'm just learning to be a nurse."

"Yes, and I must add Press, Doctor Scott said she was already as good as most doctors he knows of." The General beamed.

"Well, I'll be."

"Are you mad?" she looked worried.

"To the contrary, I'm proud of you."

"Well, I'm going to leave you two youngsters alone; this old man is tired. Goodnight."

"Goodnight." Virginia and Press chimed in together.

"He's getting old, isn't he?"

"In years maybe, but his spirit is young. Now, young lady, tell me about your studies."

"Well, Sir, I don't like to brag but I did set two broken legs and one broken arm already."

"Really, I'm impressed."

"I did, but their owners had been dead for several years."

Press and Virginia both laughed at the same time causing everyone in the room to look at them. "Well, I hate to leave but I better go relieve Bill so we can get some sleep. It'll be a long day tomorrow." Press rose from the table.

"May I accompany you?"

"My pleasure, ma'am."

Bill had just finished with the harness when Elizabeth greeted him from out of the darkness. Washing his hands quickly he made her a place beside the small fire he had going.

"You came alone?"

"Certainly, I'm a big girl now."

"This is not Philadelphia; it's dangerous for you to be out alone at night."

"May I have a cup of your coffee?"

"I'm serious, Liz, and yes, you can have some coffee."

"Mmm that's good, and thank you for worrying about me."

"Seems colder than back home, doesn't it?"

"Yes, and quieter."

"Do you wish you were back home?" Bill asked, trying to see her face in the shadows the fire put off.

"Sometimes, but I'm having fun."

"Riding in a wagon?"

"Yes, and seeing new country, and being with you."

"Why thank you." Bill was genuinely surprised at her answer.

"What about you?"

"Frankly, this is not my idea of fun, and yes, I would rather be back in Lane Manor; I'm not cut out for the west."

"You could be."

"Physically, not mentally. I belong behind my desk buying and selling, that's my life."

"Is that all our lives will be William, buying and selling?"

"No, of course not, but right now I'm trying to succeed with the business."

"From the figures in the books you are succeeding very well."

"No!" Bill raised his voice. "Grandfather has succeeded very well; I want to be bigger."

"Will there be time for us?"

"Why of course, when we return east we will have the biggest wedding Philadelphia has ever seen, and you my dear, will be the queen of the town."

"I just want to be your wife and the mother of your children." Looking at the dark haired handsome man beside her, uncertainty crept into her thoughts; why, she didn't know. He was certainly the most handsome and eligible man in Philadelphia. Rich and powerful, any girl would swoon over him. Shaking off her doubts she slipped into his arms, a place warm and safe, but lacking something.

Press and Virginia found them wrapped in a blanket chatting away when they walked up. "Coffee's still hot."

"No thanks, I'm full." Press said rubbing his hard stomach.

Several minutes of small talk passed when Bill stood up announcing it was time for them to turn in. Neither Bill nor Elizabeth saw Virginia steal a quick kiss before hurrying to catch up. Watching her out of sight, Press put out the fire then rolled into his blankets. Tomorrow would come early.

7

McSween's livery was a rundown skeleton of poles and rough cut lumber. Several rawboned half starved horses stood hip shot in the dilapidated corrals, displaying just enough energy to swish off the hoard of flies that descended upon them. Press could see several untreated harness sores on some of them, lowering his estimation of Mister McSween.

A throng of men were gathered at what seemed to be the central gathering place. "Sweet looking bunch, aren't they?" Bill whispered out of the corner of his mouth.

"Yea, about as sweet as a sack full of rattlers."

All eyes turned in their direction as they walked up, none of which showed any inclination toward friendliness. Press had never seen such a miserable looking bunch of men in his life.

"Gentlemen." Bill said, nodding in their direction.

"Say boss, is that thar Pilgrim a talkin' to us?" A snaggled tooth man turned to a robust man sitting on a barrel.

"Well yes, Jethro, I believe he is." The fat man answered.

"Ain't no critter ever called me a gentleman before." The man spit a stream of tobacco at Bill's feet.

"What can I do for you Pilgrims?" the fat one asked Bill.

"We're looking for a train heading west."

"Where you all be headin'?"

Press watched as the red started to creep up Bill's neck. Stepping alongside Bill he already knew what was coming. "I told you, west."

"Now sonny, there's a lot of west out here abouts." The remark made several of the men laugh.

A small rat of a man pushed to the front and looked up at Bill. "Big son of a gun, ain't he McSween?"

"I'd say he were, Shorty, very big." The fat man nodded his head. "Now Pilgrim, once more, where you be headed?"

"West." Bill answered, turning to leave, making sure to keep his eyes on the men.

Press spied an axe handle leaning against a post and eased over towards it. He knew it wouldn't be long before he would probably need its assistance.

"Smart aleck, ain't he McSween?" Another man put in.

"Now boys, don't be too critical of this here pilgrim. He's new to our neck of the woods and ain't had the proper upbringing yet."

"Why don't we show him?" the little man said, edging closer to Bill.

Press knew the fat was in the fire as soon as Bill started to grin. He had seen that grin in several Philadelphia brawls. Bill might be a dude from the city, but Press had never seen any man who enjoyed a good scrap like Bill did. And he was good at brawling.

Looking around Press figured they were only outnumbered about six to one. Not bad odds if Bill was on your side.

"Whar you going, Pilgrim?" McSween asked when Bill turned to leave.

"West, fat man, but to tell you the truth I wouldn't go to a pig wallow with this bunch of filth you've got here."

"That does it, Pilgrim, now you've gone and insulted these fine fellers."

That did it all right. Press didn't blink once before he was up to his eyeballs in the foulest bunch of bodies he had ever smelled. Grabbing for the axe handle, he saw Bill pick up the little man called Shorty and throw him bodily over the corral fence, or maybe through it. He didn't have the time to ponder on which as several fists were trying to get acquainted with his head at the same time. Swinging the axe handle as fast and hard as he could, he connected with several heads, but they were either empty or so full of whiskey it had no effect on them.

Seeing Bill under a bunch of bodies, Press fought his way towards them, only to be stopped by a rush of men coming his way. The way those fists were landing he figured what it would be like to fight an octopus. Things were definitely not going their way, but at the moment Press couldn't figure how to retreat with bodies hanging all over him.

Looking to where McSween was hollering orders, he was amazed to see the fat man still sitting on his barrel like he was at an opera. Things were definitely on the downslide when suddenly bodies started flying every which way, giving Press time to come up for air. Hearing McSween screaming like a madman he turned to see the biggest man he had ever seen in his life, a man so big he made Bill seem small in comparison.

"Malachi, you dumb jackass, you're fightin' the wrong ones." McSween was hollering at the giant who was dangling a man from each fist.

"Mister McSween, now you shouldn't call Malachi that name, I told you before, that's not nice." The giant advanced on McSween still holding the dangling men.

"Now, Malachi." The fat man yelped as the big man dropped the two men and picked him up.

Press knew McSween had to weigh at least three hundred pounds, all fat, but this young giant picked him up like a bag of air and was looking him right in the eyes.

"That does it Malachi, you're fired, now git!"

Sitting the fat man down gently the giant shuffled towards town with Bill and Press close behind. "Dang Press, what is he or it?"

"I think he's a man, but I'm not real sure."

"Well we owe him; I think we were getting the worst of that scuffle."

"You think?" Press looked at Bill in awe. "Now I know how a coon feels the next morning after tangling with a pack of hounds."

"I thought we were doing all right."

"You did, huh? Next time I'll just watch and let you know."

"You don't have to get touchy about it; everybody loses a fight now and then."

"Touchy, they dang near took my head off. One of them bit me; I'll probably catch lockjaw, and you say we were winning."

"Now, old buddy, I didn't say we were exactly winning, I said ..."

"Never mind, let's catch this feller, if we can, and thank him."

Catching up with the young man they found he had the size of a giant but the mind of a child. Never had they seen such a mountain of a man. After talking with Malachi for a few minutes as they walked towards town, Press convinced Bill to take him back to the hotel for a good feed. After all,

Press reasoned, he had just saved them from a good whipping, if not death.

Going by the wagon they picked up some clothes that were clean and not shredded when they ran into the old hostler.

"See you boys found McSween's all right." The hostler cackled, showing his toothless gums, grinning from ear to ear.

"So what." Bill advanced on the old man.

"Now Pilgrim, don't get mad. I warned you." He was still grinning, even with Bill's red hot face glaring down at him. "I'll bet it was a good scrap though, sure would have liked to of been there."

"He did warn us Bill." Press was grinning too.

"What you'uns doin' with McSween's idiot?"

"Thought we'd thank him for helping us out back there."

"Helped you out, did he, against McSween?"

"Yep."

"Well, you two do look like you were in a dog fight all right." The old man cackled again as he wandered off.

"Maybe you'd like a demonstration of how the dog fight went." Bill yelled at the man's back.

"Nope, been there sonny." He was still laughing as Bill and Press, with Malachi in tow, headed for town.

After enough food to fill six men, and the story of the one sided fight was retold several times, everyone returned to the wagon and started loading the trade goods the storekeeper had delivered.

"He's not much for conversation but he can sure work," Bill quipped, watching Malachi heft the heavy boxes.

"Too bad there aren't more people around here like him." Virginia stuck her head out the back of the wagon and glared at Bill.

Feeling the kindness in Virginia, Malachi took to her like a puppy to a boy. Watching him hover around her, not letting her lift anything, Press smiled. He knew only a gentle mind like Malachi's could truly feel the kindness that was in her.

"Press, what are we going to do with him?" She looked to where Malachi was packing a large crate.

"I'll try to get him a job before we pull out."
"Make sure they'll be kind to him."
"I will."
Walking to where the old hostler was swamping out the barn, Press greeted the man and started to speak.
"No." The livery man spoke before Press asked anything.
"No? I haven't asked anything yet."
"You're fixin' to."
"But you haven't heard the question yet." Press was perplexed.
"Yep, several times."
"All right, what was I gonna ask?"
"You were fixing to ask me to take in that overgrown ox over there." He pointed a bony finger at Malachi.
"Now, how did you know that?"
"Pilgrim, I'm seventy six years young and I've learnt to read a man's face real good, especially if he's fixin' to ask me something real dumb."
"Dumb?"
"You heard me right, Pilgrim."
"What's so dumb about giving Malachi a job? He can do the work of three men."
The old hostler spit a stream of tobacco, then looked to where Malachi was working. "You're right, but while he's doin' the work of three he's eating as much as six."
"I see." Press agreed, knowing the old man was right; he had seen Malachi eat. "Know anyone who might give him a job?"
"McSween, when he cools off."
"There's bound to be someone else."
"Nope."
"Why do you keep saying nope?" Press growled at the older man.
"Now Pilgrim, there ain't no use getting all het up at me. It's your own fault."
"My fault."
"You took him away from McSween, didn't you?"
"No, I didn't take him away from anybody."

"I don't see your problem anyway."

"How's that?"

"When ya'll move out just leave him behind."

"That's kinda cold hearted isn't it?"

"That's life, Pilgrim."

"Quit calling me Pilgrim."

"Well, that's what you are, ain't it? Or you wouldn't be in this fix?"

"If it hadn't been for Malachi, Bill and I would have probably got the crap beat out of us."

"Peers to me you did anyway." The old one cackled again, causing Press to grin.

"What's your name old timer?"

"Samuel P. Bennett. What's yourn?"

"Preston Forbes. What's the P. stand for?"

"Why, Pilgrim, of course."

Shaking his head, Press turned back to where Virginia was packing her medical supplies. "No luck, huh?"

"No."

"Hey Pilgrim." Press turned to see the livery man hurrying towards them.

"I'm going to strangle him if he calls me that one more time."

"You will do no such thing Preston Forbes. He's an old man."

"Well, it was a thought anyway."

Stopping in front of Press and Virginia the old hostler removed his hat and stared at Virginia. "Mister Bennett, may I present Miss Lane from Philadelphia."

"It's a pleasure ma'am." The old man bowed slightly, amazing Press.

"Mister Bennett." Virginia said, offering her hand. Looking at his soiled hands the old man refused to shake her hand apologizing. "That's all right, Mister Bennett, a working man should never be ashamed of a little dirt."

"Ma'am." The hostler shook her hand gently.

"If you gentlemen will excuse me, I'll get back to my work and let you talk."

"Now, Pilgrim, there goes a real lady."

Press never failed to be amazed at the effect Virginia had on everyone she met. Yes, she was a real lady and a genuine down to earth person as well.

"Pilgrim, I forgot to tell you in our last confab, there's a train two miles west of here fixing to pull stakes tomorrow for the west."

"I thank you, Mister Bennett, for telling me."

"If'n you hurry you can get there before dark."

"Will I need the army?" Press grinned.

The old hostler laughed and started back to the stables. "You're a corker Pilgrim, a real corker, and I'm still not taking the idiot."

Grinning, Press went to find Bill, and twenty minutes later they were on their way west to find the train. It was getting late so they put their horses into a slow, ground eating lope.

"What are we gonna do with Malachi?" Press asked as they rode.

"Leave him."

"You know Virginia isn't going for that."

"Tell her you've found somebody to take him."

"No, I won't lie to her."

"Well I'm open for suggestions." Bill quipped at Press' dilemma.

The well used wagon road led due west towards the river. Press could see the passage of many a wagon wheel. Tomorrow they would be on their way towards Fort Laramie and a rendezvous with Phillip, or Lone Eagle.

8

The wagon train was spread out all along the river. Grass was abundant and livestock roamed everywhere, watched over by a few of the older boys. It looked like chaos to Bill, but Press could see everyone was at work, excited about tomorrow's departure to the west and their future homes. Oxen, intermingled with horses and mules, grazed slowly along the river bank's deep grass. A few milk cows, some with calves by their sides, were also present in the great herd.

"Lot's of oxen." Bill fumed. "Gonna be a slow moving train."

Press nodded agreement, but for the long haul he knew the oxen would be much sturdier. Slower, yes, but they would get you to the end of the trail.

"And besides, why do we have to travel with the train? We've been doing pretty well so far!"

"By ourselves, no, we've got the girls to think about and out here there's safety in numbers." Press pointed across the broad Missouri. "Over there it's a whole new world, wild, unexplored, complete with several different hostile tribes."

Riding in, they were directed to where the wagon master had set up his camp. Several men stood around in bunches, their heads together deep in conversation.

"Here we go again," Bill remarked shaking his head.

"This time, let me do the talking."

"Fine with me." Bill agreed.

An older man in his late fifties stepped forward as soon as Bill and Press reined in their horses. A well built man with a military bearing, the man greeted the two with a firm handshake and a smile putting Bill's fears to rest.

"Benjamin Taylor at your service, gentlemen."

"Preston Forbes, and this is William Lane of Philadelphia. We're here to book passage west."

"Just you two, no wagon?"

"No, there are five of us and we have a wagon."

"Where ya'll headed?"

"Fort Laramie."

"Fort Laramie, that's about six hundred miles. Probably reach there in about seven or eight weeks with no trouble." The Captain was figuring in his head.

"That's about what I figured."

"You been west Mister Forbes?"

"Yes, I'm stationed at Fort Laramie, and just call me Press."

The Captain took another hard look at Press, then nodded. "You fought any injuns?"

"Just observed them mostly."

"Observed them?"

"Treaties and ration days and such."

"I see, but you do know them?"

"Somewhat."

"The reason I'm asking, we'll be needing a couple more scouts for the train, and I was thinking you two might work out. I guess he's army, too; officer by the looks of him." The Captain pulled out a well worn corn cob pipe and struck a sulphur to it.

"We'd be happy to oblige as long as our women folk are watched after in our absence."

"You can be assured of that."

"Anything else?" Bill asked.

"Plenty of powder and lead."

"We're well supplied."

"One other thing, I don't allow drinking or fighting on my train." The Captain studied the bruises on Bill's face. "Now, for your contract and your passage money."

"If you don't mind, we'll let the General sign us up and pay when he arrives in the morning."

"That'll be fine, but don't you want to know what I'll be a charging you?"

"We're sure you will be fair."

Captain Taylor rubbed his chin and studied Bill's face closely. "Lane from Philadelphia, I served under a General Lane, with Andy Jackson when I was just a Sergeant."

"That's the same General Lane." Bill smiled.

"I'll be, and he's out here! He must be seventy, seemed like he was a hundred, thirty five years ago."

"Don't let him hear you say that." Press grinned.

"He was a notion all right. A real pistol, fight anytime, anywhere, and didn't care about the odds. The British were scared of his colors coming down the road. I'll tell you …"

The Captain was stopped short as a buckskin clad figure rode up. Dismounting, the rider walked to where the three men stood, his moccasin clad feet not making a sound on the hard packed dirt of the camp. Press figured him for a mountain man by his bearing and dress. Slender built, not an ounce of fat on his frame, the man had a cold hard stare out of his gray eyes that were framed by a broad forehead and a full, shoulder length, head of brown hair.

"Boys, this is my chief scout, Ed Monk."

Nodding, the three men shook hands, with Monk sizing up Bill and Press with one glance. "These are your new help Ed, if you don't mind me picking them for you? I think they'll be fine."

"I've seen'em in action already Cap'n." Monk grinned.

"How's that?" the Captain was curious.

"At McSween's this morning. They had a real set to going when I rode by. I see you two kept your hair." The scout nodded his head. "They'll do Cap'n."

"By the way," the Captain pulled on his pipe. "Ya'll using horses or oxen?"

"Horses."

"Oxen are better for where we're headin'." Monk put in.

"They'll get us to Laramie."

"That where you'uns headed?" Bill nodded, but offered nothing further, and good manners would not permit Monk to inquire further.

Bill and Press mounted. "We'll be here bright and early." Waving, they turned their horses back towards town.

Virginia and Elizabeth were in the hotel room trying on different articles of clothing they had just purchased at the general store. Pulling a sunbonnet onto her head Elizabeth laughed at the way she looked in the mirror.

"You look beautiful, it mirrors your face."

"I look like a farmer's wife."

"Is that bad?"

"Not if you're a farmer's wife, but I want to stay the young belle at each Philadelphia ball." Elizabeth breathed deeply.

"A bonnet will not make you look old."

"But, what will Bill think?"

"He'll think you are smart to protect your face from the sun."

"I hope so." Elizabeth was dubious.

"You know what I would like to wear?"

"This ought to be good."

"Pants."

"Virginia Lane!" Elizabeth gasped.

"Well, they look comfortable, and think how they would show off my figure."

"Gin, you're just a little tease."

"Just for one man."

"Oh, and I suppose no other man would be able to see you in them?"

"I should hope not." Virginia laughed.

"Well, you're not, so forget it."

"Could you see Grandfather's face?"

"It would be funnier to see your face when he got through with you."

A thump at the door brought the girls back to reality, and Elizabeth to her feet, to answer the door. Malachi's large frame filled the door, packages sticking out from his large arms.

"More?" Elizabeth questioned.

"Just a few things for the boys."

Looking at Malachi's dirty, ragged clothes, Virginia set the packages on the bed and motioned for the young giant to follow her. "I'll be back; Malachi needs clothes."

"He needs a bath more than clothes." Elizabeth wrinkled her nose.

"That, too."

With Malachi close behind, Virginia crossed quickly to the general store and climbed the steps. As she entered the door, she accidentally bumped into a large man exiting at the same time.

"Excuse me, Sir."

"Well, now." The man eyed Virginia up and down. "I didn't mind at all missy."

Virginia made an attempt to go past the man, only to have his arm block her path. Seeing the trouble, the storekeeper hurried to the front door.

"Mister Logan, the lady …"

"Stay out of this, store man; I'm just talking to the lady." The man glared at the storekeeper who backed down and returned to the interior of the store.

"Get out of my way." Virginia glared at the big man.

"Now, I'm just trying to be friendly, that's all."

Turning to leave, Virginia's elbow was grabbed roughly, hard enough to make her gasp. "What's your hurry, cutie?"

Suddenly from beside Virginia a huge hand clamped shut over the man's wrist so hard Virginia could hear the bones crush from the force. Screaming the big man fell to his knees, begging to be turned loose.

"Malachi, turn him loose."

"He, he hurt Missy Virginia." Malachi stuttered still holding the man's broken wrist.

"Turn him loose, now!" She ordered, watching the man crumple, writhing on the floor. "Now, come with me!"

Several men stared in amazement as the huge Malachi followed Virginia down the steps, leaving the man rolling on the porch, holding onto his wrist. Quickly turning the corner Virginia ducked into the first barber shop she came to.

"This gentleman needs a haircut and a bath." Virginia's hands were still shaking as she opened her purse. "How much will that be?"

"Four bits, ma'am."

Paying the barber, Virginia turned to leave, only to find Malachi following her. "Sit," she ordered him into the waiting barber chair. Dubiously the barber looked at Malachi who from the look of him had never had a bath or a hair cut either. Several minutes passed before Malachi came outside with the barber right behind him, mad as a wet hen.

"What happened?" Virginia could barely hold back her laughter seeing the barber soaking wet.

"I'll tell you, I'll tell you." The barber was so mad he couldn't get the words out.

"Well?"

"Ma'am, I finally managed to get the idiots hair cut...."

"Malachi, Sir, if you don't mind?"

"Yes ma'am." Well I poured the water and told him to get in the tub and the dern fool, sorry ma'am, Malachi got in all right, but he didn't take off his clothes. I know they needed a bath too. Anyway, I hollered for him to take them off and the next thing I knew he put me in the tub."

"I'm sorry Sir, Malachi isn't use to taking baths, but if you'll try again I'll assure you that he will be good and I will make it worth your while." Virginia produced a ten dollar coin and waved it at the man.

"Well, seein's how I'm already wet I'll try one more time, but if he drowns me Madam, I'm holding you responsible. But for ten dollars I'd give an elephant a bath." The man grinned then pocketed Virginia's money.

Wagging her finger at Malachi, Virginia grinned at the funny spectacle of the big man following the little barber back into the shop. Crossing the street to another general store Virginia quickly purchased the biggest pants and shirt they had. Hurrying back to the shop, fearful of more trouble with Malachi, she smiled when she heard the sound of water splashing from inside.

Ten minutes later the barber announced the bath was finished. Virginia handed over the new clothes and waited. Malachi appeared at the door pink from the scrubbing, his new clothes tight but they were clean.

"How's that, ma'am?" the barber beamed in spite of the soap suds all over him.

"Fine Sir and we thank you for your trouble."

"No trouble, I wrestled a buffalo once, but I wasn't trying to give him a bath."

With the freshly scrubbed Malachi in tow, Virginia returned to the hotel to find Elizabeth in a state of frenzy. "Virginia Lane, what on earth happened?"

"I got Malachi a bath and some new clothes."

"A bath and new clothes didn't bring the sheriff here after Malachi."

"When was he here?"

"He just left. What happened?"

Pulling Malachi inside, Virginia had just closed the door when they heard heavy footsteps on the stairs. Taking Malachi by the arm Virginia sat the big man down against the far wall.

"Has Press and Bill come back yet?"

"No."

"Where's Grandfather?"

"At the corral with the wagon."

"Quick, go get him." Virginia propelled Elizabeth towards the door just as a loud knock resounded against the thin boards.

"Open it." Virginia ordered Elizabeth, a coolness coming over her.

The Sheriff stood in the opened doorway taking in all the occupants of the room in one glance. Stepping towards Malachi he found Virginia blocking his advance. "I've come for the idiot."

"What's the charge Constable?"

"Sheriff, Lady, and the charge is assault and battery."

"And whom did he assault?" Virginia glared at the lawman.

"Sam Logan."

"Would that be the drunk that was assaulting me when Malachi came to my defense?"

"Assaulting you?"

"Yes, or is it assault out here when a ruffian manhandles a lady?"

"Why yes, certainly but...."

"Didn't you bother to ask the store keep?"

"No."

"What kind of law are you?"

"We've had this kind of trouble with the idiot before. Who the hell are you anyway?"

"I'm Virginia Lane from Philadelphia, and this is my secretary Elizabeth Hudson, and you know Malachi."

"What is he to you?" The Sheriff nodded at Malachi.

"He is in my employee."

"Employee or not I'm going to arrest him. Now move aside."

"Aren't you going to look a little silly arresting a gentleman that was trying to protect a lady?" Clearly frustrated at Virginia's questions, the Sheriff hesitated long enough for Virginia to continue. "Wouldn't it be better for you to have all of us at your office to talk this over without arresting anyone, rather than taking the chance of arresting the wrong man?"

"Do I have your word you will bring this Malachi to my office while I round up Logan?"

"You do Sir, if a lady's word means anything here."

"Miss Lane, I assure you a lady is respected as much here as in Philadelphia."

"Really?" Virginia frowned. "Is busting into a lady's room and ordering her around called respect here?"

"All right, all right, I'll go get Logan. You be at the jail in ten minutes and bring that idiot."

Shaking his head in disgust, the Sheriff tromped back down the stairs, leaving Elizabeth slumped against the wall in relief.

"Virginia Lane, what are you going to do now?"

"I'm going to the jail with Malachi."

"You're joking, let's take the back stairs and hide him, we're leaving tomorrow."

"No, I'm facing this Mister Logan and charging him with assault."

"At least wait for William and Press."

"You go find them."

Motioning for Malachi to follow, Virginia started for the jail only to find the Sheriff waiting outside. "Well, Constable?"

"We'll go to the doctor's house."

"Why?"

Exasperated, the Sheriff glared at her. "Because Miss Lane, your employee here broke Logan's wrist and the doctor is trying to fix it."

"Very well, Constable, we'll go with you."

"Thank you. I believe that's the first thing we've agreed on yet." The Sheriff led the way down the street.

Several pairs of eyes were on the trio as they made their way towards the edge of town where the doctor's house was located. The small frame cottage was surrounded by a white picket fence. Different colored flowers, freshly watered and showing a woman's touch, filled the yard.

A small woman opened the door beneath the sign that read George Pew, M.D. "Please come in Sheriff Pond."

Thinking to herself that she hadn't heard the man's name, Virginia smiled. Pond was certainly a good name for a Sheriff that was all wet.

"Mrs. Pew, I would like you to meet Miss Lane of Philadelphia." At least he had some manners Virginia thought.

"It's nice to meet you Miss Lane."

"And you, Mrs. Pew, and I would like to introduce Mr. Malachi." Virginia looked right into the Sheriff's eyes making him blush.

"No need, Malachi and I are old friends. Malachi, you know where the milk and cookies are." The young doctor's wife smiled at the young giant, making Virginia take an instant liking to her.

"I'm sorry Mrs. Pew, Malachi is under arrest and I want him in my sight at all time."

"Arrest for what?" The small woman was genuinely surprised.

"Assault and battery."

"Come now, Sheriff. You know Malachi wouldn't harm a fly."

"Logan's wrist would probably disagree with you."

"You're taking the word of that ruffian, too?" The little woman turned to Malachi. "Into the kitchen with you now."

"Mrs. Pew." The Sheriff spoke to the woman's back as she disappeared with Malachi.

"Maybe you'd like some cookies too, Sheriff?"

"No, thank you." The Sheriff retorted as Malachi happily disappeared into the other room.

"Women are too soft hearted."

"No Constable, women just don't like to see a harmless soul like Malachi abused."

"Harmless, he broke a man's arm."

"True, but maybe he had a good reason." Virginia retorted.

"Well, I assure you I'm not going to abuse Malachi."

The doctor opened the door to his office, giving them all a sharp glance over the rims of his glasses. "Would you people step into my office; I believe Mister Logan will be more comfortable where he is."

"Well, Logan, I see you're alive." Sheriff Pond leveled a hard stare at the man.

"No thanks to her or her idiot."

"I'll need a statement from both parties, if you're able?"

"Yea, sure."

"Good, maybe we can get this mess ironed out. Now, I'm just taking a statement from both parties to see what to charge who with. Now, Logan, who attacked and broke your arm?"

"That idiot, Malachi."

"And why did Malachi break your arm?"

"Hell, he's an idiot, that's why."

"Sheriff Pond, I'll have no profanity in my home." Mrs. Pew said coming into the room.

"Yes ma'am. Now Logan, what were you doing when he grabbed you?"

"Talking to that lady there." Logan pointed at Virginia.

"Did you grab her?"

"No!"

"So, what you're saying is Malachi broke your arm for no apparent reason?"

"That's what I'm saying all right."

"Miss Lane, did you see Malachi grab Logan here?"

"No."

"She's lying!" Logan hollered, rising from his chair.

"Shut up. You've had your turn." The Sheriff glared at Logan till he slumped back into his chair.

"I broke the man's wrist."

"She's lying, I had ah …" Logan caught himself and shut up.

"You had what Mister Logan, a hold of me?"

"I had a good view of you, that's all."

"Miss Lane, did Logan grab you?" the Sheriff intervened.

"Yes."

"Can you prove that?" Dr. Pew asked.

"I'm sorry Miss Lane, the storekeeper said he didn't see anything, and Malachi's testimony is useless." Pond added.

"Well, I have a bruise on my elbow where he grabbed me that the good doctor can verify."

"Even if you do, you could have gotten it before this morning." Logan retorted.

"A doctor can tell when a bruise is just starting to color."

"And just how do you know that?"

"Because sir, I am a trained nurse."

"Really Miss Lane?" The doctor's curiosity was aroused.

"Would you check her elbow Doctor Pew?"

"This is ridiculous." Logan objected.

"You're the one who filed the assault charges."

"Well, forget it. I'm getting shanghaied here."

"You dropping your charges Logan?"

"Yea, I'm dropping them."

"And you Miss Lane?"

"Considering Mister Logan has the broken wrist I won't file any charges either."

"Good. Now, I want Malachi out of my town before tomorrow morning." The sheriff pulled on his hat and reached for the door. "And if he's not, I'll lock the both of you up tighter than a nut shell."

Stepping outside into the sunlight, Virginia watched the Sheriff disappear down the street. Inhaling deeply, she grinned broadly. She almost laughed out loud. Never had she been thrown out of a town before.

With Malachi in tow, Virginia started down the dusty street. Wagons of every kind crowded the main drag. Clanking harness and squeaking wagon wheels filled the air, along with the yelling of the team's drivers. Stepping around fresh horse droppings Virginia lifted her dress slightly and made her way towards the hotel.

General Lane and Elizabeth were just coming from the hotel when Virginia reached the front porch. Concern and relief showed on both of their faces when they saw Virginia.

"What happened, my dear?" The General put a gentle arm around Virginia.

"We're fine Grandfather; I'll tell you everything over dinner."

Press and Bill arrived just as the rest of the family was sitting down to dinner. Buffalo steaks and potatoes were in abundance. Not as fancy as Lane Manor, but the food would definitely fill a man's stomach.

"Everything's set. We pull out in the morning." Bill announced pulling up a chair.

"Fine, fine." The General answered deep in thought.

"Press told the wagon boss you would take care of the passage when we arrived in the morning."

"That's good. Now if you will excuse me." The General stood slowly leaning slightly on his chair. "Lieutenant, I'll see you in my room after you've finished eating."

"Fine, General Lane." Press stood wondering. The General never called him by his rank. Something was wrong. Virginia and Elizabeth were both subdued. Only Malachi and Bill dipped deeply into their food.

As quickly as the General went to his room, Virginia was on her feet motioning for Press to follow her outside. Stepping out into the cool night air she whirled on him tears streaming down her face.

"What's wrong?" Press was bewildered at the tears. Virginia was a strong woman; tears did not come easily for her.

"It's Grandfather; oh Press, he's challenged a man to a duel."

"What?" Press's mouth fell open. "Why?"

Virginia quickly related the afternoon's trouble with Logan, and the Sheriff telling her to get Malachi out of town, which was the same as telling her to leave town, too. Press knew this was a grave insult to a man like the General, with his pride and gentleman's attitude, towards one of his family members, especially Virginia.

"I'm surprised, knowing the old war horse, he hasn't killed this Logan already." Press grinned.

"It isn't funny Preston Forbes!" Virginia stamped her foot, annoyed at his attitude.

"Oh, Gin, you said the man had a broken arm. We'll be long gone before he heals up enough to fight any kind of a duel."

"Grandfather is going to fight. He says it's a matter of honor and he's going to fight this big bully with just one hand."

"It'll be all right." Press pulled her into his safe arms.

Hearing a commotion inside, Press knew Bill had heard the news from Virginia. Quickly reentering the hotel, they found Bill striding back and forth across the room, deep rage engulfing his face.

Glaring at Virgina, Bill towered above her. "He's not fighting any duels, much less with a man thirty years his junior!"

"What are you going to do?" Press stepped towards Bill.

"I'm going to kill this Logan."

"You can't do that!"

"And why not?"

"The General has his pride and sense of honor. For you to do his fighting would take both from him."

"That's better than him being dead."

"Would it Bill? Not for a man like the General, the shame would kill him."

"I said he's not fighting anyone!"

"You, my boy, have no say in the matter." Everyone turned to see the stern face of the General standing in the doorway. "Now, we'll talk no more of this tonight."

"Grandfather." Virginia flung herself into his arms. "It's all my fault."

"Why child, for being kind to someone; no, it's not your fault."

"But what if you're killed?"

"I'll be fine."

"You're right, Sir, because I'm not going to let you fight this stupid duel."

Hardness came into the General's face as he turned to face the irate Bill. "It may be stupid to you William. I hope not, but when a man starts letting ruffians manhandle their women folks and let them be run out of town like common trollops, he stops being a man."

"I'll fight him for you."

"No, the only thing you are going to do is take the women to meet the train. We will join you later."

"Like hell I will."

"If Press will do me the honor, he will be my second."

"If that's your wish, Sir."

"Preston Forbes." Virginia exclaimed. "You can't mean that?"

"I'm sorry Gin; it's you're Grandfather's wish."

"And what about my wishes?"

"I'm sorry."

"I'm sorry, too. I thought you loved me." Virginia stormed from the room.

"Why am I not your second?" Bill looked at his Grandfather.

"Because, William, you're too hot headed and might do something to dishonor the Lane name."

"The Lane name!" Bill spat.

"Yes, the Lane name, a name that's always been carried in high honor. No man will shame it, not even you."

"Do you think Press will stand by idly if you are killed?"

"I hope so, but he is not a Lane."

"He is the same as family."

"Yes, he is, in everything, but name. I hope you understand William, but Preston will be my second."

Cooling down, Bill nodded his head slowly. "I understand Sir, and good luck." He stepped forward and embraced the older man.

"Good, good." The General smiled, then motioned towards his room. "When you finish Lieutenant, a word please."

"Does he have a chance Press?" Bill asked when they were alone.

"He's proud, but no fool and he's been in more duels than any man we know."

"Promise me one thing."

"You have my word. Logan is a dead man however this works out, but we can't interfere, it would kill him."

"Then good luck."

"Try to make her understand and tell her I'm sorry."

"She's a Lane. She understands she just loves Grandfather so much."

Shaking hands the two friends nodded, then departed to their rooms.

9

Press found General Lane sitting quietly as he entered the room. No emotion showed on the elder man's face as he motioned Press to a chair. Pulling a card from the table, he handed it to the younger man.

"First, you will call on Mister Logan and present my card. Second, find a doctor and have him on hand at this engagement."

"Sir,"

"Yes."

"If I may, how many duels have you fought?"

"Six and I am not proud of any of them, but sometimes there is no other way."

Press left the General sitting in his chair and walked towards the saloon to find Logan. Walking slowly he tried to figure a way to stop this foolishness, but could think of nothing in the time it took him to reach the front door.

Finding the man was easy as he was the only man in the room that fit the description, and also had a bandage on his wrist. "Logan!"

"Yeah, who's asking?"

"Preston Forbes, second for General Horatio Lane."

"What's a second?"

Handing the General's calling card to the man, he thought what a waste it was to place honor on a swine like this. Logan studied the card, slowly turning his eyes towards Press.

"You mean the old geezer was serious?"

"He is."

"I can't fight an old man. I'd be the laughing stock of the whole territory."

"Then, Logan, can I tell him you decline his challenge?"

"That could be worse." Logan rubbed his chin trying to decide what to do.

"Go on, Logan, fight him. You scared?" a man in the room hollered causing several others to laugh.

"See what I mean mister? Shucks, I don't want to fight that old man."

"Then it's off?" Elated, Press turned to leave.

"Forbes." Turning, Press faced the big man. "I could fight you."

"That, Logan, would pleasure me immensely, but the General has first call on you."

"You yellow?'

"What do you think?"

"No, I can see it in your eyes. You would love to kill me now."

"You read eyes real good, Logan."

"And if I kill the old man?"

"Then, I will kill you."

"That's interesting."

"It'll get that way; you can bet on it."

"I'm not yellow either, but I'm damned if I do and damned if I don't."

"You would be alive."

"Maybe I will be anyway."

"Your gamble."

"Anything else?" Logan asked as Press turned to leave.

"Daylight at the crossing."

"I'll be there. What are the weapons?"

"You're choice."

"Let the old man pick them." The big man laughed.

"Agreed, bring your second and we'll supply the weapons."

"I'll be there."

"Logan!" Press snapped his eyes like steel.

"What?"

"Make your will. Either way it goes you're a dead man."

Leaving the saloon, Press asked a passerby directions to the doctor's house. Entering the yard, he found the doctor and his wife sitting on their front porch.

"Someone hurt?" the doctor inquired.

"I would like to procure your services for daylight tomorrow morning."

"For what purpose?"
"A duel will be fought at daylight."
"A duel!"
"Yes, between General Lane and Mister Logan."
"Lane, where have I heard that name before?"
"This afternoon, ma'am. The young girl with Malachi."
"But, I thought that was all cleared up."
"Not to General Lane; he doesn't forgive someone insulting his granddaughter."
"His granddaughter? He must be an old man, several years older than Logan."
"He is."
"Does the Sheriff know of this?"
"No, it will be at the crossing outside of town."
"I see."
"Will you be there?"
"I don't approve, but," the doctor hesitated, "if my services may be needed I will be there."
"In the morning then." Press bowed slightly to the doctor's wife and walked toward the hotel.

Back at the hotel he found the General deep asleep without a care in the world. Pure guts and rawhide, no wonder the British feared to see him coming. Crawling into his bed, Press was awakened to find the General standing over him.

"Sorry Sir, I slept too late."
"You needed it. Is everything in order?"
"He's given you the choice of weapons, and the doctor has agreed to be there."
"Good." The General smiled and nodded his head. "Sabers it is then."
"Sabers?" Press was incredulous.
"My favorite. Not too many men can face one, now we will wrap my right hand as his is wrapped."

Grinning Press laughed out loud. "You sly old fox."

"Young man, I didn't live to be this old on luck alone." The General just happened to be left handed.

The sun was rising slowly over the eastern sky, spreading its warm glow on the sandy banks of the river. Cottonwoods and sycamore shaded both banks. Birds were coming alive in the clearing near the wagon crossing. The doctor and sheriff stood to the side with a crowd of onlookers who came to watch the fun. Logan still looked as if he was feeling the effects of the previous nights drinking. The General had discarded his farmer's clothes for a dark broad suit that fit him perfectly. Where he got it Press had no idea.

"Preston, since the Sheriff is here, ask him if he would be the official rules man for this contest. That way, however it turns out, there will be no trouble with the law."

Nodding, Press walked to where the Sheriff stood. "Sir, General Lane asks that you preside over this match."

"I care nothing for duels mister, and if it were in my jurisdiction I would stop it now."

"Well Sheriff, since this duel is some of your doing, I would hope that you would try to keep it honorable and fair."

"My doing? And how do you figure that?"

"You told his granddaughter to leave town. In his eyes that's an insult of the highest order."

"I told her to get Malachi out of town. That's my duty."

"Then do your duty now and keep this duel fair."

Calling the two combatants together, after the Sheriff agreed to officiate the duel, Press gave each his instructions. "Gentlemen, we are here to settle a matter of honor. This will be a fight to the death; the weapons of choice will be sabers. Are there any questions?"

"Sabers?" Logan looked sharply at Press.

"You gave up your right to choose weapons. The other gentleman has chosen sabers. Do you wish to apologize and retreat from the field?"

"No." Logan spit.

"Very well, either combatant who uses any weapon other than the saber he chooses will be immediately shot by the Sheriff."

Pulling his pistol so both combatants knew he was serious, the Sheriff asked each if they were ready. The morning sun shined brightly from the mirrored sides of the sabers as both men raised them, ready to do battle. "Fight."

Press' blood raced through his veins with the fire of any fighting man as the two men started forward. The General moved easily out of the mad rushes of Logan, who Press could see was totally unfamiliar with sword fighting. A lunge brought Logan clumsily past the older man who used the flat side of his saber on Logan's backside, causing the big man to leap forward. Several in the crowd laughed.

"I'm gonna have your heart for that old man." Logan hissed his teeth barred in an animal fury.

The General only smiled, not speaking, parrying each thrust Logan made at him, playing with the man. A wild swing from Logan reached the General's leg, causing a spurt of blood to shoot down his boots. Press watched the old warrior's face, he knew Logan could kill the older man, but no quarter would be asked or given.

Feeling the warm blood running in his boot the General went to work. The sharp saber was cutting Logan's clothes to threads but not a drop of blood showed anywhere. In a flash Logan knew death stood before him. This old man had been playing with him. Total fear paralyzed the man, as it does most bullies when faced with their own blood. Terror reached into Logan's heart. Slashing at the older man in a frenzied state, he howled when the sharp edge of the older man's saber cut deeply into his arm. Terrified, he dropped his saber and turned to run only to have the General's saber reach between his legs and trip him. Falling on his face with the General's boot in the middle of his back, Logan screamed in terror when the saber touched his neck.

"I'll not kill you Sir, but you will remember the feel of my steel to your dying day," the General hissed, bringing the broad side of his blade down on Logans backside, making the man scream out from pain and terror. The men watching shivered as the blows rained down splattering blood with each lick. Logan tried in vain to rise, only to have the saber drive him back to the sandy ground. Shaking their heads, the men headed back to town, leaving the old man standing over their fallen hero that had passed out.

"General Lane, would you like for me to bandage your leg?"

"I wish nothing from you Doctor." The General wiped his blade on what was left of Logan's shirt, then mounted the horse being held for him by Press.

Watching the two men ride off, the Sheriff nodded his head. "They don't make em like that anymore."

"Maybe, we've all learned something today." Dr. Pew walked to where the fallen man lay. "I know Mister Logan has."

Virginia, eyes alert for any sign of Press and the General, sat on the tailgate of the large wagon. Spotting the horsemen she yelled for Bill to halt the team, and ran back down the wagon road towards them.

"Oh Grandfather, you're all right."

"Why Lass, did you think I wouldn't be?"

"I was so worried." She held tightly to his stirrup.

"Nonsense child, but I could use a little doctoring from a capable young lady."

"Are you hurt?" She quickly looked up to where he sat. "You are hurt; you're face is ashen."

"Just a scratch."

Walking around to the other side of the horse, Virginia examined the wound quickly without stopping the horse. Bill had left the team in Elizabeth's care and came to the rear of the wagon.

"What's wrong?"

"Grandfather's hurt. Help him into the wagon."

After helping the General into the wagon, Bill and Press were quickly ushered back outside. With orders from Virginia to get some hot water, they started putting a fire together.

"What happened?" Bill asked as soon as they had the fire going. Press quickly recounted the story, starting from when Bill had left, leaving nothing out.

"I'll be." Bill whistled. I sure would have liked to have seen it."

"No, I don't think you would have." Press started for the wagon with a pan of hot water. "It wasn't a pretty sight."

"Open the canvas, I'll need more light." Virginia ordered from inside the wagon.

Pulling scissors from her bag she went to work deftly on the General's pants. Quickly cutting through his boot tops, she only grinned when the old warrior started hollering about her ruining his new boots.

Cleaning the wound, Virginia found no serious damage, just a deep slash that would need stitches, one more scar to go with all the others. After sewing the leg up and wrapping it she called the men in.

"There Grandfather, you'll be as good as new in a few days, or until you decide to get into more trouble."

"Thank you, Doctor. What do I owe you?" The General joked.

"You've already paid me many times over." She leaned over and gave her patient a kiss on the cheek.

"Well now, I've never had a Doctor kiss me before." He grinned. "Maybe I'll do this again."

"No you don't, I'll give you a kiss just to keep you out of trouble."

Bill looked over the tailgate. "How are you doing Grandfather?"

"He's fine; except he's so tough the needle would hardly go through his hide."

"Preston."

"Yes sir."

"Thank you, son."

Reassured the General could travel, Bill took the reins and left Press and Virginia riding on the tailgate. Both saddle horses were tied to the wagon, and plodded along behind the slow moving Conestoga. Leaning against Press' strong shoulder Virginia sat that way a long time before she spoke.

"I'm sorry; I was just being a little fool."

"No, you were just being a caring Granddaughter."

"Thank you for being the strong one."

"You're not still mad?"

"I love you too much to stay mad long."

"And I love you, Doctor." Press smiled down at her, letting his lips touch lightly on her forehead.

Inside the jolting wagon, the General smiled before falling off to sleep. The wagon train had just finished their noon meal when the Lane wagon overtook them. Captain Taylor came riding to meet them, just as they were taking their place at the end of the train.

"Didn't miss you folks until a ways back. Trouble?"

"A little, the General needed a little patching up when he returned to the train, so we pulled up long enough for Virginia to see after him." Bill explained.

Peering at the back of the wagon, Taylor dismounted. "Nothing serious, I hope?"

"Just a few stitches."

"I didn't know you were a doctor, Miss Lane."

"Only a nurse, Captain Taylor."

"Well ma'am in that case, I'll have to confess myself. I'm just a Sergeant, but you see the folks around here think I'm A Captain, and when I start giving orders they listen better."

"I see, well then Captain Taylor."

Taylor smiled. "Yes, Doctor Lane."

"Sergeant Taylor!" A roar came from the back of the wagon making a huge grin appear on Taylor's face. Turning, the wagon master saluted General Lane who had appeared on the tailgate of the wagon.

"It's good to see you, Sir."

"Likewise, Sergeant."

"Getting a little slow, Sir, or did you forget to duck?"

"Sergeant, you always did ask too many fool questions." The General frowned, but all there could tell he had a deep fondness and respect for the man.

"Yes Sir."

"I guess you've all met Sergeant Taylor. He's the only man alive who ever called me a dang fool and got away with it."

"Frazier's Bog." Taylor beamed.

"That's where it happened."

"Was he right?" Bill asked curious.

"I was."

"Partly." The General admitted, grinning.

"We've got a train to move. I'll guarantee you'll hear all about it and plenty more before we reach Laramie." Sergeant Taylor returned to Captain Taylor and with a few yells and curses had the wagons moving westward again.

The Lane wagon, bringing up the rear, caught all the dust from the other wagons. After a few miles the elder Lane took the lines and relieved Virginia, assuring her that the wagons would rotate every day, so tomorrow they would be out of the dust for awhile.

The sun was low in the west when the train started to separate, each wagon veering to the right or left to make a great circle. All wagon tongues were pulled close together to make a holding pen for the stock in case of Indian attack.

Unhitching the teams, all the drivers had to do was pull the wagon tongues together, and it made a tight circle that would hold the tired teams even in a hard storm that sometimes spooked the animals with the heavy thunder and flashing lightning.

Supper was served and the men had started checking the wagon wheels and harness, when up and down the line they heard Captain Taylor was calling a meeting. Seeing some of the men had showed up without their rifles, he promptly sent them to retrieve their weapons.

"That, gentlemen," he said when all the men had returned. "Will be the last time I want to see any of you, from the age of fourteen on up, out of reach of your weapons."

All heads nodded sheepishly. "Good. Now let's get down to business. We've got a long way to go and some time to make up if we're gonna beat the snows through the high mountains. I've got the best trail scout, and I, myself, have been across this trail three times from start to end, so we should have no trouble."

"Captain Taylor." a tall skinny man with a bobbing adams apple spoke up. "Can we expect any trouble with Indians?"

"For now no, there has been no trouble with the tribes except for a little horse stealing and the normal begging, but we must be on guard at all times. Besides Mister Monk I have chosen Preston Forbes and William Lane to be our two other scouts for this crossing. Both men are Military men and very competent. General Horatio Lane will be my replacement should anything befall me. If anyone objects," Taylor pointed to the east. "there's the road back."

"Another thing, since you all stayed put, if these men give you an order, obey it or I'll have you whipped so fast you'd think your daddy had a hold of you. From time to time, friendly Indians will come into camp wanting handouts, so be sure before you get itchy fingers, whether they are friendly or hostile."

"How do we know?"

"You'll know, believe me."

With no more questions forthcoming, the Captain bade them all goodnight, with a warning the train would pull out at five the next morning and there would be no stragglers.

"Five?" Elizabeth made a face. "Does that come in the morning, too?"

"Yes, darling, and we have to have breakfast over, the wagon loaded and hitched up, so you'll probably be up at four." Bill couldn't suppress a grin. After all, they wanted to come.

10

Five o'clock found the train starting to move. The horses and oxen, bodies straining, pulled the heavy wagons forward, breaking wheels loose from the raw virgin earth. Hollering, cursing, and the sounds of bullwhips, echoed up and down the line. Gradually the noise subsided leaving only the sounds of the trace chains rattling. Bill and Press were flanking the wagons while Monk rode far in front watching for any signs of trouble.

The day passed slowly. Press pulled a biscuit Virginia had wrapped him and munched slowly. He could see Bill slouched in his saddle. Knowing Bill, Press laughed out loud, he knew his friend was not enjoying this little outing, and they had plenty more days just like it ahead.

Coming upon Monk at sundown, Press looked at the spot the scout had picked for night camp. A small stream meandered slowly along, and the grass was belly deep on the stock. Turning his horse he motioned for the wagons to circle, and then stepped down beside where Monk sat against a tree.

"Well, Mister Monk, that's one day."

"Yep." Monk spit a stream of tobacco at a passing stink bug.

"Are we posting a guard out here tonight?"

"No need, we'll keep close to the wagons for a spell yet."

"Haven't I seen you somewhere?" Press asked the scout in halting Sioux, and filling in with sign talk the words he didn't know.

"Well, I'll be." Monk was surprised that Press could speak the Sioux tongue. "Maybe." He replied using sign language.

"Fort Laramie, the big council last year."

"I were there all right."

"I was adjutant at the fort."

"Yep, I seed you there."

"My Sioux needs working on."

"We'll do that."

"How about tonight; take supper with us."

"All right, this old coon ain't never skipped a woman's cooking, Lieutenant."

"Press."

"Press, it is then."

Virginia and Elizabeth were not taken with the scout's manners and fire blackened buckskins the first time he took dinner at the Lane wagon, but on his next trip they started to warm to his storytelling and genuine delight of eating their cooking. He had brought each of the girls a handmade pair of moccasins, decorated with porcupine quills that made them smile with delight.

"They are beautiful." Both girls exclaimed over the moccasins.

"Put 'em on, ladies."

"Where did you get them?" Elizabeth turned them over in her hands.

"Why, I made em."

"Where did you learn such splendid work?"

"Wife."

"Wife, we didn't know you were married," Elizabeth exclaimed.

"Ain't, she died of the fever." A hush fell over everyone. "She were a Cheyenne, prettiest woman I ever laid eyes on."

"Cheyenne." Bill was curious.

"Yep, bought her from her old daddy for three horses."

"Mister Monk!" Virginia exclaimed.

"That's the way it's done out here missy."

"How about that Grandfather, how much can we get for Virginia?" Bill laughed, slapping his leg.

"William Lane; you watch your mouth!" Virginia frowned.

Monk lifted a fire brand and pulled on his pipe. The aroma settled across the night air as everyone sipped on coffee and stared into the glowing embers of the fire.

"Did you live with the Cheyenne?" Press asked.

"Yep, trapped on the Musselshell, and stayed with them during the cold times."

"What was it like?" Elizabeth asked, her eyes shining with interest.

"Free, Missy, free; go where you liked, when you liked."

"Why did you leave?" Press asked, curious.

"After the fever took her and the boy, every time I looked at a squaw or a young one it brought back too many memories."

"I'm sorry, Mister Monk." Virginia was saddened at the story.

"No need, but I thank you. No, I haven't been back to Bear Paw's camp since they passed."

"Monk," Press asked. "Have you ever camped with the Sioux?"

"Yep, most of them, from time to time."

"Did you ever camp with an Ogallala Warrior named Tall Bow?"

"Wintered with him two years, tough old heathen."

"Did you know his son?"

"Which'un?" Monk pulled on his pipe. "Got hisself two left, one got killed by the Blackfeet, couple years back."

"Tall, well built warrior, sub chief I believe, goes by the name of Lone Eagle."

"Tall Warrior they call him. Real names Lone Eagle, bad medicine that one, real bad."

Virginia leaned forward towards Monk. "Why do you say that?"

"Big medicine this Lone Eagle is. Most Sioux boys are sixteen or more before they become warriors, not this one. Counted his first coup at fourteen and had two more before he was fifteen. I know, I was there and watched them sing his praises. Yes siree bob, he's a bad'un."

"Coup?" Elizabeth quizzed the scout.

"A coup, Missy, is when a warrior touches a live enemy with his bow or coup stick in combat, and lives to brag about it. This Lone Eagle did just that, plus he added a little, their scalps; and he danced the Sun Dance when he was only fifteen, and that is a tough un. They tie rawhide thongs through your hide and you have to jerk them out before you pass out. Real fun that one is. Yep, ole Lone Eagle is bad news if'n he don't like you. Always gave me the willies when he looked at me. Kinda like a wolf looking at raw meat."

"How dreadful." Virginia shivered.

"Fascinating!" Elizabeth breathed, a glint in her eye.

"Is he really that bad Mister Monk?" Virginia asked.

"Yes ma'am, he is. One time, and this story came from Moses Harp an old mountain man who lived with the Sioux, and was present at the fight. Anyway, as I was saying, this Lone Eagle must have been about nineteen at the time, met up with a war party of Snakes, another enemy tribe. They came together on the banks of the Big Horn River. There was a lot of yelling and boasting back and forth. Then Harp said, Lone Eagle rode into the river and insulted the leader of the Snakes.

They called this one Buffalo Hump, plenty bad himself. They insulted each other pretty good, then went at it, hand to hand right in the middle of the river. Both horses went down then Harp says both men came together, but this Lone Eagle didn't even pull a knife or nothing. Just swats old Buffalo Hump, raises him up over his head, and breaks his back on the way down. Then, he up and scalps what's left; charges the rest of the Snakes on foot sending them scooting for home; and Harp swears, it's the pure gospel. If you don't believe it take a look see at his scalp pole. No sir, I don't want no part of that'un, he scares the by jiminy out of me."

"Mister Monk," Bill stared into the fire. "How old would you say this Lone Eagle would be?"

"Well, Bill." The scout looked at the younger Lane like he hadn't seen him before. Leaning forward into the shadows, he studied Bill's face for the longest. "I'd say you and him are about the same age." Rising and patting his pipe against his buckskin pants, he shrugged and looked down at Bill. "Yep, about the same age."

After the scout left Press turned to where Bill sat. "How about that, did you see the way he looked at you?"

"I saw, I was waiting for him to say something."

"He wouldn't, these old mountain men mind their own business, unless you ask them direct."

General Lane stood up and announced bedtime. Bill grabbed his and Press' bedroll from the wagon, and tossed them under the wagon.

"I'll check the horses before I turn in." Press announced, heading towards the picket line.

Saddle horses were kept close in case they were needed quickly during the night. Two men guarded the work horses and oxen letting them graze as much as they wanted.

Near the picketed horses Press sensed someone following him. Crouching silently into the tall grass he waited. Shaking his head, Press grabbed Virginia's arm as she walked by.

"Preston Forbes, you scared me half to death." Virginia whispered.

"What are you doing out here?"

"I thought you'd like company."

"Gin, I would like your company, but this is wild country out here. It's not Philadelphia; I could have been an Indian, bear, or anything."

"Well you're not, and anyway I'm armed." She held up a heavy stick for him to see.

"Ok. You win, and I am glad you came."

"Really?"

Pulling her into his arms, Press started to steal a kiss, when a twig breaking underfoot brought his attention to the surrounding darkness. Whispering for her to be still, Press pulled her down beside him.

Three men walked within a whisper of where they waited, passing towards the wagons. Too dark to identify any of them, Press walked to where the horses stood peacefully. None were missing, and everything seemed to be in order. The men must have been from the wagon train, out here checking their own stock.

"It's getting late. We best be getting back." Press said, still concerned about the three men.

"First, a kiss, then I'll go." Virginia teased.

"Well honey, I can't tell whether you're ugly, or old, but you sound kinda pretty, so I'll handle that little chore for the boy there." A voice came out of the gloom.

Press wheeled towards the sound of the voice, pushing Virginia behind him. "Who are you?"

"Just passing by Pilgrim, that's all."

"Then pass on and quick."

"Soon's I get my kiss the lady offered, maybe even two." The voice came again, but this time a large figure appeared with it.

Press felt something hard touch his hand. It was Virginia's stick. Taking a firm grip he waited for the man to move closer then brought the stick down across the man's head, dropping him like a sack of potatoes.

Grabbing Virginia's arm Press propelled her quietly into the light of the wagons. "See Mister Forbes, I do come in handy sometimes, don't I?"

"Gin, I swear you've got more nerve than sense sometimes. Those men could have been dangerous. Now get yourself in bed."

"Nope, not without my kiss." She whispered, moving closer to him."

The next morning as Press was saddling his sorrel, Ed Monk rode up from the picket line. Swinging a leg over his saddle horn, he sat there peering down.

"Morning Ed."

"Morning, fine weather for traveling."

"Sure is."

"Yep, fine weather." Monk repeated himself, while staring a hole in Press.

"How far you figure we'll get today?"

Still staring, Monk motioned with his pipe. "Twenty miles if'n we're real lucky."

"Ed, why are you staring a hole through me?"

"We had visitors last night." It was more of a statement than a question.

"Oh." Press shrugged.

"What's going on?" Bill asked walking up.

"Just this, Mister Forbes had a set to with three men last night, one larger man and two smaller ones. Apparently he came out on top as I don't see any knots on his head, and there were signs of a fight, and this." Monk said producing a small club with blood on it.

Press looked down at the stick Monk tossed at his feet.

"Boy, I can track a lizard across a skillet and tell you what he had for breakfast. From now on, I want to know everything that goes on around here. Muy Pronto." He added for effect.

"Yes Sir." Both Bill and Press answered quickly.

"You must have done for one of them good; they left out without taking any horses." Monk turned his horse and rode off.

"What was that all about?"

"I didn't think that he could read sign better than an Injun." Press grinned then walked towards the wagon.

"Where you going now?" Bill asked.

"Put this in the wagon."

"It's just a stick for pete's sake."

"It's a souvenir."

"Souvenir, are you holding something back from me?"

"Why William, would I do that?"

"Dang right you would." Bill spoke to Press' back. It has something to do with Virginia, Bill thought to himself.

11

The great black stallion pranced proudly along the banks of the Yellowstone River. A few white spots on his coat reflected brightly in the morning sun. An Appaloosa, he was the horse of the great people, the Nez Perce. The warrior on his back sat proudly, his strong back straight as an arrow. His huge chest rippling with muscle, his arms corded and bunched, every muscle coiled like steel springs. Everything about this young warrior spoke of pride, from the strong broad forehead to the piercing eyes.

The man and the horse moved as one, their eyes missing nothing as they searched the early morning mist of the river's banks. The warrior knew the horse would smell out danger long before he himself would see it. The pointing of the ears, the quiver of a nostril, or the tensing of the body, would alert the warrior to danger. In his village he always kept the great stallion tethered near his lodge. Better than a dog, he could not be bribed with meat or scared away.

Nearing the final descent to the river the stallion stopped suddenly, his ears trained forward, his nostrils quivering as they picked up the smell of strange horses. The warrior knew it could be just a band of wild mustangs, but something, or someone, waited on the far bank, hidden in the shadows of the trees.

Several riders emerged from the trees and walked their horses slowly to the river's edge. Blackfeet, their hair and facial markings identified them to the young warrior. Great and fierce warriors, a tribe of fighters as mighty as the Sioux people. The Blackfeet sat their ponies, calmly watching the stranger across the river.

Lone Eagle sat motionless, he knew the great stallion under him could easily outrun the Blackfoot ponies, but he had not come this far to run, or to fight. He was here to return the bones of his brother, so he could be honored by his village. For two years his brother, Walks Alone, had lain where he had fallen. Lone Eagle had been too young to make such a dangerous journey into the far country. Tall Bow, his father, had forbidden it. But now, he was a warrior with many coups, and he had come and he would not run. Raising his right hand palm out, he kneed the stallion forward to the river's edge. Only the swift cold waters of the Yellowstone separated Lone Eagle from the Blackfeet.

The first of the Blackfeet warriors wanting to show his courage and count coup on the strange warrior yelled his war cry and charged, sending water spraying around the legs of his lunging war horse. Racing past Lone Eagle the Blackfoot lashed out with his coup stick striking the immobile warrior across the back. Screaming his war cry, he rode back across the river to the cheers of his companions. Another came forward this time causing a trickle of blood to run down Lone Eagle's face.

Unflinching, Lone Eagle again held up his hand in a sign of peace. A third warrior raced across the river, then pulled his plunging horse to a stop beside the waiting Lone eagle. Pulling his knife he sliced Lone Eagle's arm causing a stream of blood to flow down his arm. Lone Eagle calmly stared into the eyes of the warrior.

"Why, you come here," the warrior spoke in the tongue of the Sioux. "if you do not wish to fight?"

"I have come for the bones of my brother. I have not come to fight the mighty Blackfeet."

"The one killed two summers ago when he came to raid our horse herd?"

"Yes."

"The spotted one you ride, he was taken from us that summer. He was young and unbroken, but I still recognize him."

"He is the same; my brother's warriors gave him to me when they returned."

"How are you called?"

"I am Lone Eagle, Ogallala Sioux."

"I have heard of a warrior named Lone Eagle, killer of Crows, Pawnees and Whites."

"And you?"

"Black Leggings."

"And I have heard of Black Leggings. The Blackfeet people are great warriors, and I have heard Black Leggings is the greatest warrior amongst his people."

"Lone Eagle is brave, but maybe foolish; there are many of us."

"I did not come here to fight, only for the body of my brother."

"Is his bones important enough to die for?"

"Death is better than shame; if I am to die so be it, but I will not leave here without my brother's bones."

The Blackfoot nodded his head slowly then looked to the north. "When I was very young, I was captured by the Crows. I was wounded trying to escape. A Sioux warrior named Tall Bow found me. He bound my wounds and brought me back to this very place so I could make my way to my village. Today I repay that debt, then once more we will be enemies. Come, we go."

"Tall Bow is my father."

"I did not know. I killed the son of a man I owe my life too. For this I am sad." Black Leggings shook his head.

"You fought an enemy. I would have done the same, you did not know."

The Blackfoot Warriors and the lone Sioux Warrior crossed the Yellowstone and headed north. Lone Eagle knew the spirits were with him. The Blackfeet could have killed him easily, but they respected a brave man, and they knew this one did not know the meaning of fear.

Nightfall found the band of warriors camped in a small valley ringed with steep mountains. Wild flowers gave the place a sweet smell almost like the fragrances the maidens wore back in Lone Eagle's village. The war trail had kept him busy, so he had not yet taken a wife, but still his eyes looked at the young maidens, and he knew from their shy glances that they looked back.

The Blackfoot Warriors walked around the Appaloosa Stallion and nodded their heads in approval. The horses they rode were strong, well bred animals, but they were not like this one. Nowhere in the Blackfoot Nation did such a horse as this exist.

A young bull elk had been killed and the choicest meat now sizzled over hot coals. Lone Eagle felt his stomach grumble as he had been without food all day. Thanking his hosts as they motioned him towards the fire, he cut a slice of the dark meat and returned to his seat. Black Leggings watched as the young Sioux moved with the grace of a stalking mountain cat. This warrior was powerful of build, proud and yes, even arrogant.

"You come far?"

"Yes, many suns." Lone Eagle answered between bites.

"Why did your brother come this far to take horses?" Black Leggings was curious.

Lone Eagle laid the remains of his meat aside and rubbed his hands over his forearms. "All of our people know of the beauty of the horses of the Blackfoot, and the fierceness of their warriors. He came for horses and glory."

"Your brother was young and foolish, but he was a great warrior. He took many Blackfoot warriors with him to the next life. He was a brave man." Black Leggings stared into the fire. "A very brave man."

"Yes, he was brave, maybe too brave." Lone Eagle agreed.

"You do not hate the Blackfeet for killing him?"

"No, it was a good death, a warrior's death. No, I only hate the enemies of my people, and the whites who come into our lands, and destroy our hunting grounds."

"Are there many whites in your land?"

"Not yet, but the white traders among us say they are like the leaves on a tree, many are to the east."

"I also fight the Crow, but the whites we do not see in our lands."

"You will, after they devour us they will come for you."

"Perhaps Lone Eagle is right, but now my friend, it is time for us to sleep." Black Leggings could feel the hate emitting from the young Sioux when he spoke of the whites. Maybe the Blackfeet should fear the whites.

The second day of hard riding brought the party of warriors into another valley, split down the middle by a small stream. Black Leggings stopped his pony on a small knoll. The entire valley was within their view. Lone Eagle scanned the meadows, his eyes stopping on a scaffold near the far end of the valley. Looking to where Black Leggings sat, he saw the warrior nod his head.

Kicking the stallion forward, Lone Eagle loped to where the scaffold stood. His eyes took in the once beautiful buffalo robes that covered his brother's body. The skeleton of a horse lay under the scaffold. Walks Alone's bow and weapons hung from the scaffold. Black Leggings and his warriors held back, leaving Lone Eagle alone with his brother.

The high keening notes of the death song drifted across the valley as Lone Eagle sang the song of death in respect to his brother. Rising slowly, he led the stallion to where the Blackfeet had started a fire.

"You have honored my brother, yet he was your enemy?"

"Yes, I did honor to a great warrior, a great enemy makes a stronger people, he deserved to be honored."

"For this, I thank you. If you ever need me, I will be ready."

"You will take his body from this place?"

Lone Eagle's eyes drifted over the scaffold then turned to the beautiful valley. "No, his name was Walks Alone, he would like this place. If it is good with your people he will remain here."

Black Leggings nodded. "His spirit will be remembered, his burial place will never be touched."

Lone Eagle pulled his huge razor sharp skinning knife from its sheath, and looked down at it. Taken from a white trapper, it was indeed a thing of beauty. Razor sharp, its bone handle was carved with the head of a grizzly bear. Next to the stallion it was his most prized possession.

"This knife is strong medicine for me. For what you have done, it is for you." Lone Eagle returned the knife to its sheath, and handed it to the amazed Black Leggings.

The Blackfoot Chief ran his fingers over the knife's handle. "It is indeed strong medicine, thank you Lone Eagle."

"The stallion too, he is yours." Lone Eagle looked to where the stallion grazed.

"Again, I thank you, but no, he would be of no use to me, no other could keep up with him; he will go home with you."

Lone Eagle danced and prayed around the scaffold that held his brother until morning, when fatigue finally sank him to the ground beneath the scaffold. Rising slowly, he walked back to where the warriors waited.

"Your brother was terrible in battle. What made him so?" One of the warriors asked.

Lone Eagle chewed on the meat they had given him, and remembered back to when he was only ten summers old. He slowly related the story of the Night of Death. The cold times were coming and the meat taking times had been bad. The herds had not come so the men were all away hunting. The Snake Warriors had discovered the village guarded by only the old men, and boys. There had been no warning only screaming and death.

Walks Alone had fought like a demon that day, but had been unable to save his mother from death, or his sister from capture. Death had seemed to avoid the young warrior, and his arrows found their mark time and again. Lone Eagle had seen the enemy arrows sail harmlessly past Walks Alone. The enemy had retreated, but had taken several women and horses as they left.

When the older warriors returned, the medicine man had proclaimed everywhere in the village that Walks Alone had great medicine; he would never be killed by enemy arrows. Even their war clubs and knives would be harmless against him.

This is what made him so terrible in battle. Later Walks Alone left the village alone and was gone for a full moon, but when he returned he brought back the women, horses and several enemy scalps with him. He never told, nor did the women, how he had killed so many by himself. The Blackfoot warriors mumbled amongst themselves at this story. Then they looked towards the far scaffold as if frightened. Black Leggings looked solemnly into the embers of the fire.

"The medicine man did not lie. Your brother did not die from our weapons. We were fighting there." Black Leggings pointed to a rock outcropping. "His pony fell, crushing his head against the stone."

One of the warriors spoke. "He was truly protected by the great ones. The Grandfathers wanted him in the spirit world with them, so they summoned him to come. This one, Walks Alone, was truly a great warrior."

12

The train moved slowly but steadily towards St. Joseph. The weather stayed beautiful and the girls were loving the adventure, much to Press and Bill's displeasure, as there was always an endless supply of young men around the Lane wagon.

General Lane chaffed at the bit, wanting the train to move faster. Every night, as Monk talked, he became more convinced that Phillip and Lone Eagle was the same person. The family quarrel that spurred his son to take his family west, came back more vividly every day. Perhaps, finding Phillip would ease some of the pain, take away some of the blame he had put on himself for his son leaving Philadelphia, and for the disaster that followed.

No living person knew of the terrible quarrel that had precipitated his son's departure with his wife and three children. Never as strong physically or mentally as the General or Bill, he had wilted under the constant pressure of trying to be like his father. At last his weaknesses had consumed him, and the subsequent flight from Philadelphia, west to California and death.

Getting Virginia and Bill back was a miracle in itself. General Lane had thought it was enough, but now with this new knowledge that Phillip might be found, he had to push on to find his missing grandson, if possible. Nothing short of death itself would slow him, until he came face to face with this young warrior, Lone Eagle.

Impressed with Monk's uncanny ability to read sign, Press sought the scout out every day, learning everything he could from him. No English was spoken away from the wagons, only the Sioux dialect or hand sign language. Finally Monk started leaving false trails for Press, making them harder and harder, smiling in satisfaction when Press brought in whatever he had left at the end of the trail.

Around the fire at night Virginia commented that Press was acting more and more like Monk. The two were inseparable, making her slightly jealous. Still, she knew he was learning to survive here in the west.

Alone, far in front of the train, Monk looked to where Press rode beside him and said. "I thought Bill would take more of an interest?"

"Don't fault Bill. It's just as well; he's a city man and will always be."

"I reckon so. I just don't see what a healthy young man like him would want with a city, when he could have all of this." Monk pointed at the passing countryside.

"He's just not interested."

"What's he doing out here then?"

"He would never let his grandfather come out here alone, and the General was coming. Don't cut Bill short he's tougher than boot leather."

"I'm not. It's just I figured if'n you were all going after this Lone Eagle, he could use a little injun savvy."

"What makes you think we're after Lone Eagle?"

"Now boy, don't you go cuttin' me short."

Press grinned and then related the Lane's story and why they were headed for Laramie.

"If you don't mind Ed, keep this to yourself."

"Okay, but you keep something to yourself too."

"What's that?"

"Your hair! Cause I don't think this Lone Eagle, or Phillip, or whoever he is, will wait for you to tell him your story."

"Is he that bad?"

"Worse, he's not white, he's Ogallala Sioux, and don't be forgettin' it if'n you have to kill him."

The campfire was aglow as they unsaddled and tethered their horses. Elizabeth and Virginia were bustling around getting supper ready. Elizabeth smiled as Monk moved closer to the fire. His stories of the west made her eyes light up and she was always ready to hear more. Granted some of his yarns were a little farfetched, still she enjoyed them immensely.

With Monk's stories and the unending arguing between the General and Captain Taylor, the supper fire was never dull. Bill and Press also were able to enjoy the bantering as the trail had stayed quiet and peaceful, and Monk hadn't kept them on guard at night.

"Grandfather." Virginia asked. "You never did tell us about the time Captain Taylor called you a fool."

"I was hoping you would forget and not ask."

"Then the Captain must have been right."

"I was." Taylor answered, stepping in from the shadows.

"No, you weren't, I should have had you shot."

"You almost got us both shot." Taylor retorted, a huge grin on his face.

Exasperated, the General shook his head and turned his gaze on the fire. Virginia wasn't about to let this good a story slip by. Turning to Taylor she was about to ask him to tell the story when the General spoke up.

"If it's got to be told I'll tell it; at least it will be half accurate." The old General smiled.

"I wouldn't tell a windy." Taylor protested.

"Uh huh. Well, let's see now. It was in July, hotter than an oven. We had engaged a large party of Creek Indians at a place called Frazier's Bog, a bad marshy piece of land, hip deep in mud and flies. Anyway, we whipped them good, had them on the run we did with our boys in hot pursuit, when I tired of all the mud on me and decided, much to Sergeant Taylor's displeasure, to have myself a bath.

"Yes Sir, with hostiles everywhere." Taylor quipped.

"What happened then?" Virginia leaned forward.

"Nothing, I took my bath and went back to camp."

"That's not quite what happened." Taylor grinned wider, as the General turned beet red.

"You tell us, Captain." Virginia couldn't wait.

"I certainly will, your grandfather, General Horatio Lane, was facing the bank of the creek. I wasn't watching behind me like I should have been doing. Anyway, as calm as if he was in church he asks me to get our uniforms. Well when I turned around, our uniforms just happened to be lying at the feet of about the maddest, meanest, and orneriest looking bunch of injuns you ever seen. Then he asks me if I knew what an honorable retreat looked like, and I allowed as I didn't he proceeded to show me. We made a hasty retreat out of there swimming as fast as we could. And we had a lot of help hurrying. Arrows and everything else they could throw at us including a little rifle fire just missed our bare backsides.

Your Grandfathers luck as usual helped us, as a bunch of our lads showed up just in time. But, they took our uniforms and somewhere today there's two injuns wearing a General's uniform, and a Sergeant's uniform. And what's worse, thanks to the General's pride, we had to walk buck naked through the whole dang command. And I can tell you, there was a lot of snickering and down right laughing, going on all around us. And Missy, that's the gospel.

"Grandfather, you didn't." Virginia laughed until her sides were about to bust.

"Sergeant Taylor, I might have you shot yet."

Nothing tonight was going to best that story, so everyone turned in. The last thing heard was Bill roaring with laughter, after he got over the shock of his aristocratic grandfather naked in front of his troops.

Noon the next day found the train halted on the banks of a small but fast running river. The scouts had come in to help with the crossing. A storm, up river, had swollen the river until it was almost out of banks and very dangerous. Much discussion went on amongst the men, whether to cross or wait for the water to ebb. Busy talking, no one noticed the small band of warriors watching the train from the nearby buttes.

"Cap'n, we got company." Monk motioned towards the watching Indians. Taylor studied the horsemen, then decided to circle the wagons for the night.

Trying to cross now, and maybe being attacked, would be foolhardy. "What tribe?" He asked Monk.

"Too far to be sure, maybe Cheyenne."

"Too far east for Cheyenne." Taylor lit his pipe and studied the butte.

"Yes usually, but not for a raiding party."

"General, set up camp as usual, but be ready for anything. Keep the stock inside the wagons and shoot the first man you see without his rifle." Taylor ordered.

"Well Sergeant, maybe you should have been the general."

"Not a chance; I don't like baths." Taylor had to get one more jab in at the General.

The warriors had disappeared from the buttes and the sun was low in the west when they reappeared, this time riding single file towards the train. The leader circled his horse several times as they rode up to the wagons.

"What do you think, Ed?"

"Cheyenne war party for sure, maybe wanting to trade. We'll find out pretty quick."

"Ed, you and Press come with me; Bill you and the General have everybody ready, but don't let anyone get a nervous finger and shoot."

Meeting halfway between the two groups, a warrior greeted the white men and started gesturing with his hands. Press was pleased that he could follow the hand talk easily.

"What'd he say?" Monk turned to Press, curious if his student had learned his lessons well.

"They've been on a raid, got a couple of their men hurt, wants to know if we've got a white medicine man."

Monk nodded. "That's it in a nutshell, Captain."

"What do you think, Ed?"

"If the girl can patch them up we might make a few friends, and we've got a long way to go across their country."

"Press, see if Miss Lane will patch these bucks up."

Press loped back to the circled wagons and quickly summoned Virginia and the General. Press had quickly explained the situation to Virginia, and she had just grabbed her medical bag when Bill rode up.

"What's going on?"

"Got themselves a couple of hurt men, Gin's going to patch them up."

"The devil she will!"

"William," The General's calm voice spoke easily, "she'll be all right, and it may do the train a service."

Press tied his horse and carrying Virginia's bag they walked back towards the warriors. Bill, with Malachi close behind, followed. The large warrior motioned, and a horse pulling a travois was brought forward.

Monk spoke a few words then motioned towards Virginia. Several of the warriors shook their heads, and gave the cut hand sign for no.

"What's the commotion about?" Confused, Taylor looked at Monk.

"Squaw." Monk answered spitting a stream of tobacco on the ground. "I don't think they'll let her fix'em, bad medicine."

"Nonsense!" Virginia brushed the big warrior aside and knelt beside the travois. Pulling a dirty trade blanket from the man, she ignored the grumbling and studied the bloody wound. Rising, she walked between the warriors to where a young warrior leaned weakly against his horse. His left arm dangled uselessly from a make shift sling. As she reached for the arm, the young warrior pulled back feebly. Stepping forward she spoke soothingly, looking the warrior straight in the eye.

"She's got nerve." Monk whispered quietly to Press.

"Tell him I can heal his wounds."

A tall warrior started forward menacingly, only to be blocked by Malachi's huge frame. "Tell him." Virginia repeated.

Monk nodded at the warrior and translated her words. Dismounting, the Chief stepped in front of Virginia, and stared quietly into her eyes. Monk repeated again she was a medicine woman and could heal the warrior's wounds. Nodding his head the big warrior spoke a few words, and all of the others backed off a few steps, all the while keeping their eyes on Malachi.

"I'll need these men brought to my wagon."

"Whoa now, missy!" Taylor frowned. "I can't be having all of these bucks loose near the wagons."

"Captain Taylor, these men are hurt bad. I can't work on them out here on the ground."

"Alright, but I don't like it."

Monk translated her wishes again, causing a stir amongst the warriors. Exasperated, Virginia stepped in front of the chief looking up into his dark eyes.

"Translate this, Mr. Monk. Tell this Chief these men are bleeding to death while he and his men are arguing over everything I say. Now, if he wants me to help them, do as I wish or treat them himself." Virginia was fuming, causing a smile to come to the big warriors face. "Tell him!"

"I don't know, Miss Virginia." Monk knew this chief was a big man in the Cheyenne Villages, and he didn't want the whole Cheyenne Nation down on the train.

"Press, tell him exactly what I said; we don't have time to argue or these men will bleed to death."

Monk started translating her words before Press could decide. Virginia stepped closer to the big warrior and stared him defiantly in the eye. Monk, expecting the worst, was surprised when the Chief nodded his head in agreement.

"Now, tell him I would like for him and one other to come with us and help; the others must remain here."

The Chief nodded and motioned the others to stay behind. Virginia spoke to Malachi, and to the amazement of the warriors, he picked up the wounded man and carried him as easily as if he were a feather. Placing the man on a cot in the wagon Malachi stepped back and let Virginia have room to operate.

Motioning for the two warriors to hold the man down, Virginia pulled a scalpel from her bag. Seeing the sharp instrument, the second warrior said something to the chief; but as there was no reply, Virginia started to work on the unconscious man.

Only a few moans came from the patient as Virginia extracted a bloody arrowhead from his shoulder. Quickly sewing the wound closed, Virginia wrapped the shoulder tightly in clean bandages, then satisfied with her work she stepped back outside to where the other man waited.

This warrior, only a boy, had an ugly slash from a sharp weapon, and it had broken the upper bone in his arm. Virginia offered the young one laudanum to kill the pain, but he refused. Shrugging her shoulders, Virginia, with the help of the two warriors, set the bone back into place. Not a sound came from the young man as she stitched the wound together and applied a splint.

"Tell the chief I want both men to stay here so I can watch over them, for fever."

A quick exchange erupted between the two Cheyenne, then the Chief spoke to Press. "This warrior is the father of the young one; he wishes to stay with his son."

"If it is all right with our chief he is welcome."

"How'd it go?" Captain Taylor asked, as Virginia finished.

"Providing there's no infection from blood poisoning, they're young and strong, they'll make it."

The Cheyenne Chief started to speak to Press, then stopped abruptly as Bill walked up. Stepping closer, he studied Bill's face several seconds before retreating back to where his warriors were camped. Several of the warriors looked towards the wagons as the Chief spoke to them.

"Well now." Monk spit a stream of tobacco. "He seems to have known you, looked like he'd seen a ghost or something."

"He was looking you over for sure." Press agreed.

Cook fires blazing, Taylor figured a friendly gesture could help things along if the wounded men didn't make it, so he had the women folks of the train fix extra food for the waiting warriors.

"One thing an Indian can do better than fight and that's eat." Monk grinned, watching the warrior's wolf down hot biscuits and hoecake smothered in molasses.

Several times during the night the young warrior moaned, bringing Virginia to his side. The fever Virginia was expecting didn't set in, and by morning both wounded men were awake and noticeably stronger. Virginia had fallen asleep when Press stepped quietly into the wagon. Only Malachi and the young patient's father heard him enter.

"You walk quiet for a white eye."

"How is your son?"

The older warrior looked to where his son rested. "Your medicine woman did well for my son; he is stronger."

"This is good."

"Is she your woman?"

"She soon will be."

"You must pay many horses for her."

Press grinned. "No, whites do not buy their women."

"Then you steal her?"

"No."

"Then, how she your woman?"

"Whites marry their women."

"Indian marry too."

Exasperated Press tried to explain. "White women marry who they want to."

"Strange way, Indian way better."

"How are you called?" Press wanted to change the subject.

"I am Crow Foot."

"My name is Preston Forbes." Press extended his hand.

"The strange one watches you as close as he watches me." The warrior released Press' hand nodding at Malachi.

"He watches over the medicine woman closely."

Press stepped back out into the morning sunlight and took a cup of coffee from Bill's extended hand. Looking into the wagon, Bill laughed as Malachi looked at him sharply.

"Something, amusing?" Press asked.

"Oh, I was just thinking, you might be the first bridegroom in history to get his neck rung, trying to kiss his bride."

"Now, that's a possibility." Press chuckled.

13

Elizabeth had the breakfast fire going and coffee boiling when Virginia emerged from the wagon. Taking the coffee cup Elizabeth extended to her, she sat down tiredly on a wooden crate.

"Nothing smells as good as coffee early in the morning." Elizabeth smiled. "You handled that well last night."

"I was scared to death."

"It didn't show, everyone is proud of you."

The men came to the fire from where they had been harnessing the horses making ready for the river crossing. The small creek had gone down during the night, and Captain Taylor and the General were eager to get the train moving.

"How are your patients?" Taylor asked pouring himself a cup of coffee.

"Weak, but they'll make it."

"We've got to be moving, and I think the way them Injuns are keeping watch on their back trail they are wanting to high tail it out of here too." Monk spoke between gulps of coffee.

"They are in no shape to ride, it'll kill them."

"We've got to move now." Taylor insisted.

"Just one day, Captain Taylor."

"Lass, we can't hold the wagons one minute."

"Okay, Captain, but the wounded men must ride in the wagon so I can look after them."

"I doubt if they'll leave them." Monk spoke up.

"Tell the Chief if they ride they'll die."

The Chief, who Monk learned was named Two Dogs, a big man in the Cheyenne lodges, walked into the circle and Monk interpreted Virginia's words to him. They were all surprised when the Chief called Crow Foot from the wagon and spoke quietly with him.

"What's he saying?" Taylor asked Press.

"He asked how the wounded are, then he told Crow Foot what Virginia said."

The Chief turned back to the fire and nodded at Monk.

Monk grinned. "Well Captain, reckon you were wrong, the Chief here says the men owe the medicine woman their lives and they would do whatever she says."

"I don't believe it." Taylor shook his head.

"It's the gospel, but only the young one and his father is staying behind, the other one will be leaving."

"Tell the Chief we'll take care of the lad until he's able to ride, then we'll send him home."

Monk translated the words to Two Dogs then the Chief launched into a long oratory. When he had finished there came a roar of approval from the gathered warriors.

"What now?" Taylor asked when the uproar died down.

"They wish to show their gratitude to the people of the train for their good hearts towards the Cheyenne." Press translated.

"And?"

"Well Captain, there will be a feast tonight in honor of Miss Virginia."

"Great, more time lost." Taylor grumbled.

"To refuse would be an insult."

"Okay, tell him tonight when we make camp."

The train moved out slowly, headed west with the scouts spread out in front of the wagons. The warriors had disappeared ahead of the train and were not seen all day as the train plodded on. Monk rode a swing around the wagons then pulled up beside the wagon where Virginia was riding on the tailgate.

"You done a remarkable job back there, young lady."

"Why, thank you Sir. I had a good teacher."

"Yes, you surely did." Monk kicked his horse in a lope towards the front of the train.

An hour before sundown Monk circled his horse several times calling Press and Bill in, then headed back to the dust cloud that hovered around the train. Pulling in beside Captain Taylor and the General he spit a stream of tobacco juice before speaking.

"Them Cheyenne got themselves a fire going over that far knoll. We can circle beside the creek."

"You reckon everything will be alright?"

"Cap'n, them Cheyenne think that girl is big medicine. They ain't about to let anything happen to her."

"Kinda got 'em eatin' out of her hands, huh?" Taylor grinned.

"That's a fact, for sure."

The evening turned into a gala atmosphere. The Cheyenne had brought in several deer and the choice cuts from a buffalo. The women fixed bread and desserts. Guards were placed at intervals around the wagons, and to Taylor's amazement, Two Dogs had some of his own men standing guard. A fiddle was produced and a lively dance started with several of the Cheyenne putting on a show of their own. When the music slowed a huge Cheyenne warrior stepped into the firelight and motioned to where Malachi sat. Monk knew what was coming, and quickly moved to where Press sat.

"They want to wrestle Malachi."

"No!" Virginia exclaimed.

"It's just in fun, missy." Monk grinned. "Nobody will get hurt."

Press walked to where Malachi was sitting and kneeled beside the big man. Malachi was nervous as the warriors were pointing at him and motioning him forward. "They want to wrestle with you." Press explained. "Do you understand?"

The giant nodded slowly then stepped forward to where the Indian was waiting. Press wasn't sure Malachi understood wrestling, but when the big man motioned for more warriors to come forward he grinned; this might be a good show as long as no one gets mad.

Three warriors rushed Malachi with a whoop grabbing his arms and waist, trying to get him down. Try as they would, they couldn't move the big man an inch. Suddenly, Malachi flexed his big arms and lifted two of the Cheyenne clear off the ground, then flung them loose like they were children. The third Cheyenne released his hold and shook his head in amazement. Laughing, Two Dogs stepped in, and slapped Malachi on the back. Launching into a fiery oratory the Chief spoke a few minutes, then waited for Monk to translate.

"The Chief is thanking all of you, and now he wants to pay honor to the newest member of the Cheyenne Nation and his daughter." Monk turned to where Virginia was standing and motioned her forward.

Monk presented the astonished Virginia to everyone, then stepped her in front of Two Dogs. The Chief removed a beautiful silver medallion from a deer skin pouch, and placed it over Virginia's head.

"I couldn't, it's far too much." Virginia turned the medallion in her hands.

"Take it Lass, and smile; you don't want to insult the Chief."

Virginia smiled, and as the Chief spoke Monk translated his words. "He says, now you are his adopted daughter, cousin to the mighty Sioux, and to wear this medallion at all times, as it will tell all the people that you are protected by Two Dogs of the Cheyenne Nation. If you do this you will never be in danger from the people."

The Chief stepped back and the young warrior with the broken arm led a chestnut mare forward and handed Virginia the braided rawhide rein that held her.

"For, me?" Virginia was truly shocked.

"For you, Lass." Monk grinned.

"She's beautiful." Virginia smiled stroking the mare's neck. "Thank him for me Ed."

"How about a ride, Miss Lane?" Press lifted her up on the back of the little mare much to everyone's delight. Virginia turned the mare and loped her in circles in front of the wagons. Monk and Press laughed when the Chief said Virginia was indeed a Cheyenne as she rode as good as any warrior.

The dancing and feasting lasted late into the night until everyone turned in exhausted. The Captain fussed and fumed; he was sure no one would feel like moving come morning. Daylight found the Cheyennes gone. Only Crow Foot and his son remained.

Monk spoke briefly to Press and Bill as the train rumbled forward. "From now on gentlemen, we watch for anyone, red or white."

"Is something wrong?" Bill queried.

"Maybe, maybe not. Two Dogs informed me before he pulled out that we were being followed by shod horses. That could mean white men or horses stolen by Injuns. I'm staying to the rear of the train so you two are on your own up front, so watch your hair."

"You heard the man." Press grinned at Bill. "Watch your hair."

"Yes sir." Bill waved as the men separated.

The wagons traveled hard all day, stopping only for a quick meal at noon. The ground was flat and hard, letting the animals set a good pace. An hour before sundown, Taylor waved his arms and the wagons began their circle. No water was near, so this would be a dry camp.

Monk split the scouts up into shifts, so one man would be circling the wagons all night. Taylor posted enough men around the wagons to keep them well guarded. Press thought the animals should be brought into the circle for safety; but he knew they needed to graze to keep up their strength. Passing Monk before heading to the supper fire, Press swung his leg around his saddle horn and studied the herd of horses being guarded by the older boys.

"You too, huh?"

"I've got an uneasy feeling, Ed."

"Yea, me too, but I ain't seen nary a thing all day."

"I'll see you at two." Press left the older scout studying their back trail.

Press caught another horse and tied him to the wagon. He didn't want to be left afoot if trouble started.

"When is Bill coming in?" Elizabeth asked handing Press a plate of food.

"I'll spell him at ten; where's the General?"

"With Virginia, checking on one of the children. I'll leave Bill's supper beside the fire. Tell him, will you?"

"I'll do that. How are you liking the trip?"

"It's wonderful out here."

"It's that." Press agreed. "I take it you don't miss Philadelphia."

"No Press, I don't." Elizabeth was frank. "But Bill does, and I'll go back with him."

"Will you be happy?"

"It's funny you should ask, because I've asked myself the same question."

"You two are sure serious tonight." Virginia could sense their serious mood as she walked up.

"Just talking, but now I've got to get some sleep."

"Press, could you speak with the boy?"

"Is something wrong?"

"No, I don't think so; just have a word with him before you go to sleep."

"Anything, for my favorite girl."

"Am I your favorite girl?" Virginia smiled up at Press.

"Wait until I return, then I'll answer that."

The dark eyes of the youth studied Press as he eased himself onto a seat beside the young Indian's bed. Beads of perspiration dampened the boy's head. "I am Press Forbes."

"I am called Raven. Have my people gone?"

"All but your father; he watches our horses."

This caused a smile to come to the face of the youth. Seeing Press looking at him, he answered the unasked question. "My father is one of the greastest of horse raiders against the whites, and now he guards your horses."

"Is he to be trusted?"

"You would believe my answer; yes, my father is an honorable man. He says we owe the medicine woman and her people much, so he will stay until she is no longer in danger."

"Is the medicine woman in danger?"

"This is dangerous country, many tribes travel it and they are not Cheyenne or Sioux."

"Can I get you anything?"

"This lodge does not let the sun come in."

"Tomorrow, you will ride in the sun."

"That is good, thank you tall one."
"Raven, have you ever seen a warrior called Lone Eagle?"
"Yes, I have seen him, many times."
"Would you tell me of him?"
"It would be better if you ask my father of this one."
"Tomorrow then, you will sit in the sun."

Press stepped down from the wagon to find Virginia waiting. Taking her arm gently, he guided her into the shadows of the wagon.

"What did he want?" She asked.

"The wagon is too hot and dim. I told him tomorrow he could ride in the sun. Indians, especially young ones, are not used to being cooped up inside for very long."

"Yes, the sunlight will do him good."

"Now, about my favorite girl; any complaints?"

"Only one, I never get to see you anymore." Virginia pouted.

"Soon, we will have the rest of our lives together."

"Is that a proposal?"

"Pretty close."

"When will it get closer?"

"The time will come."

"Soon I hope."

"I promise."

"And I will hold you to that promise." Virginia slipped into his arms. Feeling the passion from him she pulled back. "Goodnight Sir."

Press smiled down at her. "Goodnight."

14

The train rolled westward; other than a broken wheel or an animal losing a shoe, everything was smooth traveling. Raven's cot was set on the tailgate of the great Conestoga wagon where the young Indian could enjoy the sunshine.

Malachi had taken to playing with the young children every night. Virginia worried at first, then seeing the gentleness and care he took with them she relaxed. Supper had just been finished and Virginia and Elizabeth were cleaning up, when they heard one of the children cry out in pain. Running to the source of the crying, they found Malachi bending over one of the children.

"He hurt, Missy."

"Its okay, Malachi, let me see." Quickly examining the whimpering boy Virginia found he had a broken arm. "Bring him, Malachi."

"Keep your hands off my boy, you brute!" The boy's hysterical mother raced to her son, and hovered over him.

"He has a broken arm, Mrs. Young."

"My poor baby."

"I was going to have Malachi carry him to my wagon."

"It's that brute that broke his arm."

"Now, Mrs. Young, we don't know that."

"I do, and my husband will take care of him."

"Mrs. Young, your son needs attention now." Virginia was starting to lose her patience.

"I'll bring him; you keep that thing away." The mother gathered the crying boy into her arms and followed Virginia to her wagon. A little candy and thirty minutes later, the arm was set and wrapped in a splint.

"There Jimmy, in a few weeks you'll be as good as new when the splint comes off. You come back tomorrow and let me look at it, okay."

"Okay, Miss Virginia." The boy looked up at her and smiled.

"Tell her the idiot broke your arm."

"Mrs. Young, really!"

"You keep that overgrown freak away from my children, do you hear?"

"Very well, I'm sorry you feel that way."

"If he comes near Jimmy again I'll have him thrown from the train."

"That'll be quite enough madam, now leave." Virginia's patience had finally vanished.

Watching the woman depart, along with a few bystanders, Horatio walked to where Virginia was closing her medical bag. "Sometimes, people get unreasonable when their children get hurt."

"It was an accident."

"I know that, my dear, but she's still a protective mother."

"You're right Grandfather."

"It'll be forgotten tomorrow." Horatio hugged Virginia.

The General could not have been more wrong. Not an hour passed before Captain Taylor was at the Lane wagon with half the mothers on the train. Horatio could tell by the look on the Captain's face he wasn't enjoying his job.

"General, the good mothers of the train want me to tell Miss Lane that Malachi will no longer be allowed to play with the children."

"That's pretty strong, isn't it?"

"I'm sorry, Sir, but that's the way it'll have to be." Taylor cleared his throat, clearly embarrassed.

"Very well then, Captain, your orders will be carried out. Malachi will stay away from the children."

Malachi stayed close to the Lane wagon, only leaving when accompanied by Virginia or Elizabeth. Virginia could only shake her head in sorrow as she watched Malachi sit and watch the children playing in the evenings. Many people had come to rely on Virginia's medical skills, so she always had Malachi carry her bag when she visited a patient on the train. This caused a lot of tongue wagging, but not one person dared confront her.

Two weeks passed and the wagon train was making good time. Captain Taylor called for a day of rest on Sunday, so the teams could rest and be re-shod, and the wagons wheels could soak in the nearby stream. Several of the children were playing near the water. Malachi watched from where he leaned against a tree.

"When we get to Fort Laramie you will have plenty of children to play with." Virginia tried to cheer him up.

"I hurt Jimmy."

"You didn't mean to."

"The lady said I did."

"She was just upset, she didn't mean it."

"Can I play with them a lot?"

"Yes, you can; now I'm going to help Elizabeth with supper, you stay here until I call."

Virginia and Elizabeth were just finishing supper, and waiting for the men to come in, when several terrifying screams followed by a loud roar brought their attention to the children playing near the water. A large grizzly was splashing across the river in pursuit of the running children, closing in on the slowest little girl. Fear froze everyone watching; they knew they could not reach her in time.

Then, Virginia saw the fast moving form of Malachi moving in between the bear and the little girl. The young giant flung the helpless girl from danger and turned to face the enraged bear just as the grizzly reared on his hind legs and grabbed Malachi with his powerful teeth. Screaming in rage and pain, Malachi managed to tear the bear loose only to have the huge animal swat him with a powerful paw. Rising from where he had fallen, Malachi and the bear came together again, locked in a terrible death struggle. Virginia was only dimly aware of the General and Raven racing towards the deadly battle. Raven's strength gave out, and he collapsed before reaching the combatants, but the General raced on armed only with his sword.

The grizzly, intent upon mauling Malachi, was not aware of the General as he raced up and swung viciously at the bear's neck. Dropping Malachi, the grizzly turned his attention on the General. Blood from Malachi, and now the bear, was spurting everywhere. Malachi, with his life's blood pouring out from the bears mauling, managed again to throw his mighty body against the bear knocking him sideways away from the General. Ripping away from the powerful grip of Malachi the grizzly snapped his mighty jaws onto Malachi's ripped face just as the General plunged his sword through the beast's heart. Roaring in rage and pain, the bear bit at the sword protruding from him, then toppled backwards landing beside the prone body of Malachi.

Virginia had raced towards the desperate battle, only to be stopped and held by a man trying to keep her from danger. "Let me go." She screamed, slapping at the man.

"Wait, Lass."

"Damn you, let me go."

Kneeling beside Malachi, Virginia cradled his huge head in her lap. She knew at a glance Malachi was beyond help. Even with Malachi's great strength the bear was too much, he had done his deadly work. "Oh Malachi." The tears dropped on Malachi's bloody and torn face.

"I sorry Missy; did Malachi do bad again?"

"No Malachi, you're the kindest man I ever knew." Virginia sobbed.

"I didn't mean to hurt Jimm...." The huge head rolled to one side before he could finish.

"I know you didn't, you couldn't hurt anyone."

"He's gone, Lass." Horatio touched Virginia's shaking shoulder.

Every hat was removed, and several women cried, as they clutched their children, maybe some in shame at how they had treated the man who had just saved their children.

"Bravest thing I ever saw."

"Amen, fought like a demon even after he was dead."

"I never saw the like, gave his life for the little ones."

Virginia's tear streamed face looked up at the gathered people. "He was just as good and kind when he was alive."

Press, Bill, and Monk rode up just as Horatio was helping Raven back to his bed. Seeing the blood all over Virginia, and the tears running down her face, he flung himself from his horse and gathered her into his arms.

"Oh Press." Virginia cried, sobs racking her small body.

Press looked to where the crowd had parted, giving him a view of Malachi and the grizzly. "He was my friend." Virginia tried to regain her composure.

"I know, Gin."

Raven rose from his bed and looked towards the water, then back at Press. "The strange one was surely touched by the great spirits, to defeat a grizzly. The people will hear of this and sing his story for all time."

"Maybe, he was." Press agreed.

Malachi was buried on a small knoll overlooking the stream where he died. Bill had carved a marker with his name and his deed on it. Several women had come by after the ceremony and apologized to Virginia, but apologies would not bring Malachi back, nor would bitterness. She knew they would remember the brute that couldn't play with their children, but had become their angel of mercy, giving his life to save theirs.

The next day the train left Malachi behind; only a small figure on a chestnut mare remained, staring down at his marker. From a distance Press watched as Virginia turned and rode slowly after the train.

Two weeks found the train nearing Chimney Rock, Nebraska Territory, when more trouble struck. In spite of all precautions several head of horses were run off just before daylight. A loss of this magnitude would bring the train to a halt, unable to move forward without horses to pull the wagons. Several warning shots from the night guards put the train on alert, and brought the scouts on the run. What were left of the horses and oxen were rounded up and placed inside the circle.

Monk, with Press and Bill rode a distance from the train where Monk dismounted, studying the tracks by lantern light. Looking up at one of the night guards he spit a stream of tobacco.

"Tell the Captain, it were whites, probably five or six, can't tell for sure. Tell him we'll get em back."

The three, with Monk in the lead, rode out in the early morning darkness, hoping they were going right. Their horses were fresh, and ready to run. Daylight found the scouts ten miles from the train. The horses had tired, so Monk pulled to a halt, letting the horses blow. Press's sharp eyes picked up the dust cloud of the stolen horses.

"There they go boys." Monk had also seen the dust.

"They're sure careless, running those horses and stirring up all that dust." Press shook his head.

"Well, horse thieves aren't the brightest, or they wouldn't be horse thieves." Monk spit, his eyes ablaze. "Boys, lets go get our horses."

The scouts passed the herd, their horses running hard, ears flat, nostrils flared, heart's beating hard. With all the dust and noise Monk knew they wouldn't be noticed. Press was amazed at the transformation in the scout. No longer was he a wagon scout; now, he had become a hunter of men. Swinging back in front of the herd Monk slid from his horse, and crouched in a small ravine.

"Get set boys, we're gonna have ourselves a turkey shoot." The scout laughed, checking the priming on his rifle.

The three scouts spread out, their rifles resting on the lip of the gully. The tired herd was coming in at a slow trot. "Don't shoot until I do, and don't miss."

The dust was boiling around the heavy feet of the workhorses, and the riders never knew they were in danger until the roar of Monk's rifle knocked the first one from his saddle. Press and Bill fired knocking two more to the ground. The last two threw up their hands knowing they didn't have a chance. Press had reloaded, but held his fire. Monk squeezed another shot off knocking the fourth man from his horse. The last man, seeing his only hope was to run, turned his horse and whipped him into a hard run.

"Shoot him, Press." Monk bellowed, hastily reloading his rifle. "Shoot him, for pete's sake."

Suddenly a rifle roared at Press's elbow, and he watched the last rider fall from his saddle. Press turned to where Bill was lowering his smoking rifle. The cold gleam in his friend's eye made him shake his head.

"Why didn't you shoot, boy?" Monk looked puzzled at Press.

"Useless murder, Ed. They had quit."

"Mister, when they stole our horses they put every man, woman and child in danger. That didn't bother them, and killing that scum didn't bother me one bit."

"No, it didn't seem to bother either one of you, to kill those men in cold blood."

"I'll tell you this one time, mister; out here you either get tough or die. Personally, I don't think you've got the guts."

Seeing trouble a hair's breathe away, Bill stepped between Press and Monk. "Boys, there's been enough trouble today; let's go home."

Turning to his horse, Press slammed his foot hard into the stirrup, and started gathering the tired herd. Not a word was said on the return trip. Press could feel the closeness he had felt for Monk had slipped away with the death of the men. Five men lay unburied where they lay, and nothing could erase that memory.

A cheer went up from the people as the herd stumbled dead tired into the wagon circle. Press headed directly to the Lane wagon and started unsaddling without a nod to anyone. Virginia, feeling something wrong, laid her hand on Press' arm, but didn't ask. He would tell her when he was ready. Captain Taylor rested the train another day, then put the wagons on the trail, pushing them hard, trying to make up for the lost days. Press scouted ahead, but stayed to himself speaking very little.

15

The trading post at Fort Laramie came into view of the wagon train in the early summer of forty nine. The train would continue on to California and Oregon, but the Lanes and Press were at the end of their journey. The long trip was behind them; now, the search for Phillip or Lone Eagle would begin. Press looked to where Bill was riding beside Elizabeth and wondered if finding Phillip was worth losing the best friend he would ever know. Horatio and the girls had felt the coldness between the two men since the return of the work horses. Nothing had been said, everyone hoped whatever had happened would work itself out in time.

In 1849, Fort Laramie was just a small garrison with two troops of dragoons. The fort's main objective was to protect the wagon trains heading west, and dispense trade goods to the Indians. The trains stayed only long enough to re-supply. The heavy snow in the Sierras was foremost on their minds and no one knew how early they would arrive.

Press rode ahead to the fort to report to his superior officer. Several dispatches were clutched in his hand as he entered the small headquarters building.

"What can I do for you?" a young private asked noticing the buckskins Press wore and figuring him for another trapper.

"I'd like to see Colonel Dodd."

"State your business!"

"Tell the Colonel, that Lieutenant Forbes is reporting in with dispatches from the east."

The private stood to attention and saluted. "Yes Sir, sorry Sir, I didn't recognize you in that get up, I mean clothes."

"It's alright private, just tell the Colonel I'm here."

A few seconds passed before the orderly returned and motioned for Press to enter. Pulling the door to behind him, Press walked to a small desk where an older gray headed officer sat. "Lieutenant Forbes reporting, Sir." Press saluted snappily.

"Mr. Forbes," the salute was returned. "I see you made it back."

"Yes Sir."

"Any trouble?"

"No Sir."

"At ease Lieutenant, sit down." The Colonel motioned to a chair.

"Your dispatches, Sir." Press handed over the small bundle of mail.

"Good, good." The Colonel smiled. "I was running out of reading material."

"And these, Sir, are for you." Press handed over a box of Horatio's finest cigars.

"Well now, these are a sight for an old soldier's sore eyes." The Colonel smiled, lighting up a cigar immediately.

"General Lane' compliments, Sir."

"General Lane? You don't mean General Horatio Lane, Andy Jackson's fighting General?"

"Yes Sir, the same."

"I wasn't aware that you knew him."

"I know him well; he practically raised me."

"That's why you went to West Point."

"Yes Sir."

"Cigar, Lieutenant?"

"No thank you, Sir."

"And why would the old gentleman send me a box of cigars?"

"I imagine, Sir, the General knows how a soldier on post duty in the west would appreciate a good cigar."

"He's right there. I wish I could thank him personally."

"If you wish, Sir; he's outside the gates, waiting your permission to bring his wagon inside for the safety of the ladies."

"General Lane is here!" The Colonel was astounded. "And, with ladies?"

"His granddaughters, Sir; it's a long story."

"I'm sure it is Lieutenant. Let's not keep the General waiting."

Introducing the two old warriors, Press was amazed that the Colonel had never before met General Lane. Saluting sharply, Colonel Dodd gave Horatio all the military courtesy of a superior even though the General was retired. Press left the two men talking and walked to where Virginia was waiting near the wagon.

"Well, we made it, Gin."

"Isn't it beautiful?" Virginia waved her arm towards the surrounding countryside.

"Very."

"A person could fall in love with the west."

"I don't think Bill feels that way." Press nodded towards Bill and Elizabeth.

"No, he doesn't like it here at all."

"No, but Elizabeth does."

"Yes, I believe you are right."

The General and Colonel Dodd walked to where Press and Virginia stood talking. Motioning for Bill and Elizabeth to join them, Horatio introduced everyone. The Colonel bowed gallantly to the ladies and shook hands with Bill. "General, your ladies have to be tired from their journey; perhaps you all could join me and my officers for supper this evening."

"Well, thank you Sir, we would be delighted."

"Good, good, we can finish our discussion then. In the meantime the ladies can rest and I'll have a bath prepared for them." The Colonel bowed again. "Until six then."

"We'll be there."

Press and Bill drove the wagon into the fort and backed it in next to the officer's quarters. Press stripped the harness and saddles from the horses, then put them into a corral by themselves, while Bill unloaded the girl's trunks. Baths were made ready for Virginia and Elizabeth and the best dresses they had brought with them were taken out to be pressed. Bill and Press, with Raven in tow, walked to the river for their bath.

"It looks cold." Bill muttered touching his toes to the water.

"Coming down from the mountains, it probably is."

"A Cheyenne would plunge in head first and never shiver." Raven spoke up from the bank.

"What'd he say?" Bill asked shivering.

"Said you're doing fine." Press lied.

It felt good to at least be saying a few words to Bill, even if there was still a coldness between them. Press had missed his talks with Bill more than he had thought.

"A Cheyenne swims much better than a white man." Raven spoke up again.

"Yes, and I know an Indian that's gonna get a free bath if he says one more word." Press warned.

"The Medicine lady would not like that, I think."

"What's he ranting about?" Bill asked.

"He says you swim gracefully."

"I don't speak Cheyenne, but I know he's not bragging on my swimming."

Raven watched curiously as Bill and Press dried off and put on clean clothes for supper. Both took turns with the razor, much to the amusement of Raven."A Cheyenne scalps much closer than that."

"How would you like these two white men to scalp a Cheyenne named Raven?"

"I don't think the Medicine lady would like that either."

Lunging at the youth, Press laughed as Raven sprinted for the safety of the wagon. "He seems to be stronger than we thought." Bill grinned.

"He's well, just waiting around for something, I guess."

"What?" Bill asked.

"That's what Gin asked. I think he doesn't want to leave her yet. I really don't know."

The Lanes were pleasantly surprised at the fine supper they were served in the officer's quarters. All the post officers were present, each trying his best to talk the ladies ears off.

Press smiled, watching Virginia actually enjoying herself for the first time since Malachi was killed. He also knew how lonely men become for a white women's conversation on a post like Fort Laramie and didn't mind sharing her for the evening.

16

The train was re-supplied, and the day following their arrival it was ready to head west. Press was tempted to take Virginia and go with them, but duty and his dedication to the General prevented him from giving the matter another thought. The Lanes and Elizabeth walked to the train to say goodbye and wish the train luck, leaving Press and Raven behind. Press could not bring himself to say goodbye or shake hands with Monk, so he decided to wait behind at the fort.

Already the sun was up and hot. Flies swarmed everywhere lighting on everything, so Press decided to take Raven and walk to the trader's store. Finding themselves a seat on the porch out of the sun they watched a game of kickball being played by some Indian boys. Raven had started explaining the game to Press when a commotion erupted inside the store.

An old Indian landed almost at Press' feet, followed by two trappers who planted a couple of hard kicks to the old ones ribs. "That'll teach the old heathen some manners, huh Lou?" The shorter of the two men cackled.

The larger man only glared at Press and Raven, then returned inside the store without a word. Press stepped down from the porch and helped the old man from the dirt. A warning from Raven turned Press around to face the store.

"Well now, what do we have here?" The bigger trapper was standing in the doorway.

"Peers to be an Injun lover to me, Lou." The other trapper emerged from the store.

"Nah, just a Pilgrim who don't know any better."

"Be careful, Tall One," the Raven whispered. "These are two bad whites."

"Sounds like that red cur is giving him some kind of warning against us." The smaller man grinned, his broken teeth showing like a wolf's.

"Now, why would he warn anyone about two gentle, easy going fellers like us?"

Press had pushed the old man behind him, out of harms way, if trouble started. This seemed to arouse the two trappers more. "Pilgrim, you got about one second to put that Injun back where you found him." The little trapper called Ab advanced on Press.

"Or what?" Press asked evenly.

"Well, I reckon I'm gonna put you and him both back in the dirt, maybe even permanent."

Setting himself as the smaller man advanced, Press swung a wicked right that smashed into the trapper's jaw, sending him flying back onto the porch. Seeing the man go limp, Press knew the man would be out for a spell.

"Now Pilgrim, that was real unsociable of you." The one called Lou hissed, pulling his skinning knife. "Now I'm gonna cut you real bad."

Press stepped backwards giving him time to pull his own knife from his boot top. The two men circled each other warily, both looking the other over carefully before lunging in. Indians hearing of the fight seemed to come out of the woodwork. The trader walked out on the porch and looked down at the one called Ab. He had seen too many fights between these rough mountain men to take sides, or interfere. Press was unaware of the audience, his whole attention being on the trapper waving the pig sticker at him.

"You ready to bleed, Pilgrim?" The big man grinned.

Press circled craftily watching the trapper's eyes. Suddenly, as swift as a striking snake, the big man lunged, cutting a slit in Press' buckskin shirt. "Be careful, Tall One, he is good." Raven warned.

"He's not gonna help you, Pilgrim."

Press avoided the next lunge, but the third cut a long slice down his left arm. The big trapper was good. Press knew every move he made was going to have to be accurate if he was going to survive the man's onslaught. Never in his life had he fought a man with a knife, except in the river, nothing like this. A lunge from the trapper brought them face to face, each with a hold on the other's wrist. Press felt the man's brute power and knew he was no match in strength so he tore loose and stepped back.

"What's the matter, Pilgrim?" Lou grinned. "Ain't scared are you?"

Press moved like a cat, cutting a gash across the man's ribs causing only a wolfish grin to come to the man's face. "Not bad Pilgrim, not bad."

The trapper lunged in furiously, his blade swiping the air where Press had just been. Complete insanity seemed to possess the man as he followed Press across the yard. Press stepped in as the man lowered his blade, only to see his mistake as the man's blade cut clean to his ribs, bringing a shower of blood running down his shirt. Knowing he was bleeding bad Press lunged again only to receive another wound to his arm. His fighting instincts fully aroused, Press fought back with a fury only a true fighting man possessed.

A grim smile crossed his face as his blade started to find its mark. The bigger man was stronger, but Press found he was faster. The big trapper steadily retreated across the yard as Press attacked. No fear showed in the man's face but he knew death waited if he made a mistake. Both men were bleeding and starting to tire. Slamming together, Press felt the big man's blade bite into his shoulder.

With the last of his strength Press plunged his blade low, plunging it into the man's soft stomach, then twisting it sideways, gutting the man. Stepping back, Press let the big trapper sink slowly to the ground. A bewildered look crossed the big trapper's face. Feeling his head go light, Press fought the black cloud coming across his eyes just as strong arms wrapped around his waist and supported him.

"Let's go to the wagon, old friend." Bill looked down at Press.

Maybe, it was his unstable eyes playing tricks on him, but Press could have sworn there were tears in Bill's eyes. Looking at his friend, Press nodded and smiled, knowing they were once again friends. Leaning heavily on Bill, Press made it to the wagon before passing out. Raven had hurried ahead to tell Virginia of the fight and to prepare her for the shape Press was in. Forgetting she could not understand him, he climbed into the wagon to get her medicine bag, pointing to where Bill was helping Press.

Seeing Raven with her bag, and looking to where he pointed, Virginia studied the two approaching men and the way Bill was supporting Press. When she noticed the blood, it took all of her strong will to fight the hysteria clutching at her breast and to get control of her emotions. The moment passed and the self assured part of Virginia took over, directing Bill where to put Press and hollering for Elizabeth to bring hot water.

Several hours later Press woke to the sounds of drums in his ears. Looking to his side he saw the quiet face of Raven watching over him. "What happened?"

"Aiyee, the brave heart one is back among the living." Raven smiled.

"Was I dead?"

"Almost my friend, but you killed the evil one."

"Evil one?"

"The big trapper." Raven arose from where he sat and looked outside, nudging Bill who was dozing on the tail gate. Returning to Press he squatted against the cot.

"What's all the racket with the drums?" Press asked.

"Medicine man, make big medicine for Ishta Shakota."

"For who?"

"Ishta Shakota! You!"

"Mighty Heart!" Press was puzzled.

"Yes, the Sioux people have given you new name, mighty name for a mighty warrior." Raven beamed.

"Well Press, you're awake." Bill grinned.

"Awake and hungry as a bear."

"That's good, means you're gonna live."

"Was there any doubt?"

"Some, how are you feeling?"

"Sore, hurts to move anything."

"I don't doubt that. Virginia put enough stitches in you to make a quilt."

"Reckon she's pretty mad?"

"Some, she calmed down soon as she saw you were going to make it."

"Those trappers didn't leave me much choice."

"That's what the trader said; I told Virginia it was them or you."

"Raven said the trapper was dead."

"Don't come any deader. You made quite an impression on the Indians." Bill grinned.

"How's that?"

"Taking up for one of them, against a white man."

"I don't like to see an old man get kicked around in the dirt, no matter what color he is."

"I know old friend. You always did have a chivalrous streak in you."

Virginia stepped into the wagon and shooed Bill and Raven out. Setting beside him on the cot, she looked closely into his eyes, then ran her hand slowly across his unshaven face. Laying her head on his chest she sobbed quietly. Rising up, she kissed him slightly on the lips then dried her face. "Someone is here to see you."

"Who?"

"Ed."

"Monk!" Press shouted, wondering what the scout was doing back.

"Do you want to see him?"

"I'd rather see you. But it's okay."

"You'll have me forever."

Virginia stepped to the back of the wagon and motioned for Monk to enter. Hesitantly, the scout approached to where Press lay.

"Heard about the ruckus, and come back to check on you. Hope you don't mind."

"I don't mind at all."

"Boy, there's been mighty few times in my life that I've ever had to apologize, or ever wanted to. This is one of them times."

"Ed, there's no need."

"Yes, there is. I was wrong, and you're not gonna let me off without I apologize." Monk grinned.

"Yes Sir."

"I've been around too many scoundrels, for too many years and I didn't recognize a good man when I seed one, and I'm seeing one now."

"Thank you."

"Well, anyway, here's my hand, if'n you'll accept it." Monk said putting out his hand. Press reached with his good arm and took Monk's hand.

"Thank you, Press."

"No, Ed, thank you for coming back."

"We weren't far, and when I got word I lit out back here."

"Who told you?"

"I was scouting when I ran into the dead man's partner; the one you knocked cold."

"He told you what happened?"

"Somewhat, but not the way it really happened."

"How's that?"

"The way he made it sound, you got the jump on poor old Lou Larouche and killed him from behind."

"I see."

"I got the straight of it from the store man, down at the post."

"The dead man's name was Larouche."

"Yep, and a mean un."

"Canadian?" Press asked.

"French Canadian, meanest man with a knife I ever knew; well, anyway, he was once."

"Guess I was lucky."

"Not as how the Indians tell it."

"No?"

"Nope, said you took a ton of steel, then grinned and cut old Lou's stomach out. Got themselves a name for you now."

"I heard." Press was starting to blush again.

"Ishta Shakota, the mighty heart one, and from the way they explained the fight I'm inclined to say it's a good name for a brave lad."

"I was lucky."

"I would have liked to have seen it. Lou took a friend of mine with a knife once. T'was his own fault; we warned him. Well Press, I reckon I better be getting back to the wagon before the Captain skins me."

"Monk, I too, was wrong. I know now what you were trying to tell me. Out here there's only one law, and for now we make it ourselves."

"I'll see you in the spring thaw, if you all are still here."

"We'll be looking for you, and the door will be open."

"One more thing." Monk stopped. "Remember, one time I told you I didn't think you were a match for Lone Eagle."

"I remember."

"Well, just maybe, I was wrong there too. See you in the spring, and good luck to you."

Press listened as the sound of Monk's horse' hoofbeats left out of the fort. Dozing off he wasn't aware of Virginia returning to set by him. She studied his steady breathing, then assured he was okay, she stepped out of the wagon.

"Can we see him now?" The General and Colonel Dodd were waiting as she emerged.

"No Grandfather, he's asleep and needs his rest."

"Fine, fine, but is he going to be alright?"

"He's going to be fine." Virginia assured the two men.

During the week that Press was laid up, Bill rode out every day not returning until after dusk, dead tired and frustrated. For all his efforts, he had been unable to get a lead on the whereabouts of High Meadow's village. At the mere mention of a warrior named Lone Eagle, the Sioux he encountered turned a deaf ear. He wished he had taken more interest in learning the language, or at least some sign language. Raven had flat refused to accompany him. Crow Foot had gone along, but Bill knew it was more to keep him safe and out of trouble than to help find the village.

Returning from a fruitless day of searching, Bill was surprised to find Press sitting on a wooden crate beside the wagon. "Well now, I see Doctor Iron Britches let you escape from your prison." Bill smiled.

"She did, after a little fussing. One more day on that bed and I would have grown roots."

"I'm glad you're up and around."

Bill handed the reins of his horse to Crow Foot and found a crate to sit on. "Find out anything?" Press was curious.

"I swear Preston, it's like looking for a ghost, you mention Lone Eagle and everybody clams up."

"Give me a few days, and I'll be able to ride with you."

Press and Bill had been talking idly a few minutes, when a group of warriors rode up to the front gate and stopped. Sitting quietly on their mustangs, they were the wildest looking bunch of warriors Press had ever seen. A slender young warrior, dressed only in breechcloth and moccasins, swerved his horse easily around the surprised sentry and charged towards Bill and Press. Pulling his pony in hard, he stared closely at Bill for several seconds, then whirled and rode out the gate at a dead run. Stopping his horse in a slide, he turned and gazed back at the two baffled men, then with the other warriors following, rode to the traders post.

"Well now, what do you make of that?"

"Wanted a closer look at you, I reckon."

"Why?"

"Curiosity, I'd say. Probably heard you've been looking for Lone Eagle and wanted to see you for himself."

"Maybe, I'll just have me a talk with him." Bill started to rise.

"No, wait."

"Why?"

"For one, you don't speak the language, two them boys look pretty rough, and may not want to talk."

"You're the boss."

"That young one that come in here, he was something; arrogant, proud, he could be the brother to Lone Eagle, the one Monk spoke about."

"You may be right."

"I think Lone Eagle sent him in to look you over."

"What'll we do?"

"We'll wait; around Indians patience is a virtue."

"I don't feel too virtuous." Bill studied the trader's post where the warriors milled.

"They're a handsome and proud people."

"They were handsome alright, and very thrilling," Elizabeth said walking up, still staring at the warriors, a flush to her cheeks.

"Out here I don't think it would be appropriate for a young white woman to be swooning over a bunch of heathens." Bill frowned at Elizabeth, irritation showing on his face.

"I was just making a statement, not swooning." Elizabeth consoled Bill, placing her arm in his as they walked off.

Press knew by the way Bill walked he was annoyed with Elizabeth, and wondered how their relationship was doing. Funny thing, Press thought to himself, how two friends can become so close that each almost knows what the other is thinking. Sensing someone behind him, Press turned to find the old Indian he had befriended against the trapper, a large ornamental pipe across his arm. Giving the friendship sign, he motioned for the old one to sit down.

"Welcome to my camp, Grandfather." Press greeted his visitor.

A smile showed slightly on the face of the old one. "You speak the people's tongue."

"Yes."

"That is good. A man should be able to speak to his friends. I am called Lame Bull."

"It honors me to be called your friend, Grandfather."

"It honors the Sioux to have such a friend as the mighty Ishta Shakota. No white has ever befriended a Sioux as you did for me."

"Thank you."

"I have brought the pipe of peace, so that we can look into each others hearts."

"Again, I am honored."

Press watched as the old warrior packed the pipe with tobacco from a small pouch at his side. Lighting the pipe, he offered it to the four winds, then passed the pipe to Press. Nodding slightly when Press smoked and handed the pipe back, he placed it across his lap. "You had a good teacher, you know of our ways."

"Yes, he was a good teacher."

"That is good, out here a man needs to know much."

"Could I ask Lame Bull a question?"

"What is it you wish to know?"

"The young warrior who came to the gate, who was he?"

"He is Wild Horse, son of Tall Bow, and nephew of High Meadows, Chief of the Ogallala Sioux."

"He seemed very curious about my brother Bill."

"The Look Alike One."

"Why do you call Bill the Look Alike One?"

"It is a name." Lame Bull stalled.

"The Sioux have a meaning for all names."

"Yes, that is true."

"What does this name mean?"

"He looks like someone."

"Lone Eagle?" Press asked. "The other son of Tall Bow."

Hesitating, the old one stared quietly towards the trader's store where the group of warriors were milling their horses, then slowly nodded his head. "Do you know we seek the warrior, Lone Eagle, as our brother. We mean him no harm."

"Yes, I know, Raven has told me everything."

"Would you tell me of Lone Eagle?"

"Yes, but I warm you. No good will come of this; take your people and go back east from where you have come."

"Why? We only wish to talk."

"I fear the one you seek will kill you."

"He may be our brother."

"No, Lone Eagle is Sioux. He would never call the whites brother or friend.

"Perhaps we can change his mind."

Raising to his feet, the old one placed a soft, beaded, buckskin shirt in Press' lap. "You are a brave man, my son, but no, you will never change Lone Eagle. If you stay it will end badly. Come to my lodge, we will talk."

As the old man walked away Press smiled. With Wild Horse coming in he knew Lone Eagle could not be far away. Now, it was only a matter of time for him to heal before they could search out the village of this High Meadows.

"My, we're deep in thought."

"Gin, sit down please, I was just thinking."

"I noticed. What a beautiful shirt."

"Lame Bull gave it to me."

"Chief Lame Bull?"

"Yes." Press pointed to the figure of the old warrior walking out the front gate of the fort.

"Tell me, why would he give you such a shirt?"

"He was the one I helped at the trader's post."

"I see." Virginia quickly folded the shirt and placed it back on Press' lap, a frown across her face.

"It was his way of thanking me." Press added.

"And if you had been killed?"

"I wasn't."

"You could have been."

"Gin, that's enough. Things are different out here."

"I don't see any woman wanting her man to get cut to pieces."

"Good afternoon."

"Grandfather!" Virginia stammered. "We didn't hear you come up."

"Sorry, hope I'm not interrupting anything?"

"You're not, I was just leaving." Virginia said looking down at Press. "As for you, Mister Forbes, I think it's time for you to return to bed."

"In a bit."

"Don't keep him long, Grandfather."

"Fighting again, my boy?"

"Yes, Sir, she just doesn't understand some things a man has to do, if he's a man."

"She knows; it's just she was so worried."

"Well anyway, thanks for saving me a good tongue lashing."

"I've been getting acquainted with the villagers since you've been in bed, but so far I've come up with nothing."

"I've hit on something from Lame Bull just now."

"What?"

Press quickly related what he had learned. "High Meadows village has to be close."

"Good, when can we start?"

"I should be able to ride in a week."

"We're getting close; I can feel it in these old bones."

"General, don't be surprised by how this turns out. This Lone Eagle may be a hard one to get near." Press warned.

"If he's a Lane, the Lane blood in his veins will make the difference."

"I hope you're right."

"I'm right, I'll stake my life on it."

"You probably are, General."

"I see Virginia's off to the village again, I best go with her." Horatio rose to go.

"What's she doing in the village?"

"Doctoring, they've taken quite a liking to her. Even the bucks let her doctor on them."

"What about the medicine man?"

"He is not real happy, but Lame Bull keeps him in line. He must have been a real warrior in his day; his people all respect him."

"Well then, Sir. I guess I'll just ease back to bed. I'm not as strong as I thought."

"I want you to know, we're all proud of you, me especially. Wished you had of been there when we fought the Red Coats. We would have had a time."

Press watched as the old General walked towards the village, his back ramrod straight, and his walk still smooth. If Lone Eagle was truly Phillip with this old warhorse's blood running in his veins it could indeed get interesting.

17

Lone Eagle sat relaxed, his broad back against the backrest in his father's lodge. Smoke from his clay pipe curled lazily up towards the smoke hole of the lodge. Today the young warrior was deep in thought. His brother Wild Horse and other Sioux warriors had been to the trader's post at the white man's fort. They had brought back strange news of the Look Alike One, the one who had been asking for Lone Eagle.

Absently he reached for a live coal to relight his pipe. Muscles rippled as he moved. Never had the Sioux people seen a warrior like this one. It was said by the people, and even his enemies, that this one possessed great powers, the strength of a buffalo, quickness of a mountain lion, and the courage of a grizzly. The trophies of war hanging in the lodge would confirm that he was truly a great warrior.

The white one who asked for him, and looked like him! Why did he come from the east seeking Lone Eagle? Why? Lone Eagle did not trust any white, now one had come looking for him. Deep in thought he did not hear his father, Tall Bow, enter the lodge.

"You mind wanders today, my son."

"Yes, my mind is greatly troubled by the words of my brother who has just returned from the trader's store."

"I have heard the talk."

"Why do these strange whites ask for me?"

"This I do not know, but it is said they are of good hearts towards the people."

"Bah, they are white. Whites do not have good hearts, towards anything."

"The squaw they call the medicine woman cares for all the people of Lame Bull's village and asks for nothing in return."

"Yes, I have heard this."

"The one they call Ishta Shakota risked his life to help Lame Bull."

"This too, I have heard. Wild Horse said the Cheyenne, the one called Raven, is a friend of this white."

"Perhaps, these are good whites."

"No, Father, whites only take from the people, drive the game away, spread disease among our women; there are no good whites."

"Will you go to the trader's store and see this one they say looks the same as you?"

"Wild Horse has seen this one."

"Lone Eagle should not believe the things he has not seen for himself."

"My brother, Wild Horse, is my eyes. He has never told me wrong; I will not go."

"Lame Bull says they are good people."

"Lame Bull is an old man."

"Lame Bull was once a great warrior and leader."

"That was long ago; now he is a tame Indian."

"Maybe he knows something we do not."

"What?"

"The whites have many guns that shoot far. They are great warrior's maybe we should move closer and learn their ways."

"Never will I kiss the feet of the whites, never!"

"Never is a long time, my son."

"The whites have nothing I want."

"Then why does Lone Eagle sit in a dark lodge so deep in thought?"

"I would know how they know my name, and why they ask for me."

"This I cannot answer either." Tall Bow shook his head.

Lone Eagle shrugged his shoulders and looked at his father. "The scouts will soon leave to locate the buffalo."

"Yes, the meat taking time is near, the cold winds will come soon and drive the buffalo south."

"Perhaps I will take Wild Horse and ride with them."

"Yes, this would be a good thing."

Rising, Lone Eagle left the lodge and walked through the village, too deep in thought to hear the people call out his name or see their smiles. Many wondered why he did not take a wife. His horse herd was large, he could take any woman he wanted but none touched him; his eyes did not return twice to any of the younger maidens, perhaps another village. Many had shared his blankets; widowed women, their husbands killed in battle or on the buffalo hunts. This was permitted; in return the warrior would supply meat to their lodge.

Nearing the lodge of Blue Thunder, the tribe's powerful medicine man, he turned away heading for the stone hills above the village. Today he did not care to listen to the wizened old healer. Passing several young boys busily at work making arrowheads from the granite rock, he smiled remembering when he used to come to this same place for the tips of his arrows that he would send in flight after the ferocious rabbits and sage hens.

Looking across the river, he nodded in appreciation at the young men racing their war ponies up and down the sandy banks of the river. The water splashed on their horse's flanks, and the young men howled jubilantly when their charges unhorsed an opponent. No other warriors, except maybe his hated enemies the Crow, rode as well as these warriors. A lone horseman left the mock battle and rode to where Lone Eagle watched, pulling his lathered horse to a halt almost on top of the waiting warrior.

"My brother must be troubled for him to walk when he could ride. Perhaps a pretty maiden worries Lone Eagle?"

"Perhaps."

"Or maybe Lone Eagle plans a raid against the Snake dogs?"

"Maybe, Wild Horse asks too many questions."

"How else is one to learn?"

"Be quiet and listen."

"When has anyone known Wild Horse to be quiet?" The laughing youngster laid back on his horse and roared, making Lone Eagle forget his troubles.

Wild Horse was his brother's pride, a fun loving young man always in trouble with the women of the tribe, easy to laugh, but brave in battle. While everyone wondered why Lone Eagle ignored the maidens of the village, they guarded their girls from Wild Horse. A wild streak ran in the blood of the young warrior, and only time they said would cool it.

"Let us go to the land of the Snakes and take their horses and women."

"Do you not have enough women here my brother?" Lone Eagle grinned at the mischievous youth.

"I do not wish to keep their women, just borrow them."

"There are plenty of widows here."

"Bah, old squaws sap a warrior's strength." Wild Horse laughed.

"And a Snake woman does not?"

"My brother, the great Lone Eagle, grows fat and lazy, perhaps."

"Wild Horse yaps like a coyote."

The youngster threw his head back and laughed, his white teeth shining in the sunlight. Lone Eagle wondered how one so young, could be so fun loving, but so terrible in battle.

"Maybe you are right."

"Aiyee, you will see my brother." The elated youth whirled his horse around Lone Eagle.

"First, I will speak with High Meadows, our chief."

"And I will ask for warriors to follow the great Lone Eagle, but I will tell them they must give the plumpest squaw we catch to you my brother." Again Wild Horse laughed as Lone Eagle dumped him from his horse. Lying on the ground laughing, Wild Horse watched his brother walk towards the village.

Returning to the village, Lone Eagle went straight to the lodge of his uncle High Meadows, Chief of the Ogallala Sioux. Finding High Meadows sitting beside his lodge, Lone Eagle found a place beside him. "May I have a word with you my Chief?"

"Certainly, Nephew."

"My heart is heavy today. Perhaps a journey to the south would bring the good feeling back into it again."

"Perhaps."

"If a few young men hurry they would be back in time for the buffalo hunt."

"If they hurried." High Meadows agreed.

"Some good Crow buffalo horses would help the hunt."

"Where would you find these horses?"

"Perhaps, on the Sweetwater."
"This place is many moons from here."
"Yes, many, but that is where the best horses are to be found."
"Also our enemies, the Crows."
"They have the finest horses."
"They also have fine warriors."
"Not warriors like the people."
"No."
"Then do I have your permission to go?"
"Yes, make the people proud and return safely."
"Thank you Uncle."

That night Lone Eagle sat in front of his lodge while different warriors stopped by and laid their arrows on a blanket at his feet. The arrow was their pledge to join him on his venture against the Crow. Any arrow not picked up meant rejection for the owner. Each arrow had its own markings, identifying the owner. So great was Lone Eagle's reputation, that he had the number of warriors he wanted quickly. Gathering up the blanket that held the arrows, he entered his lodge. Wild Horse had been waiting inside and counted the arrows.

"My brother did not ask for many warriors."
"To raid for horses, only a few are needed."
"That is true, but only ten?"
"Maybe Wild Horse needs more to protect him. Does he wish to remain behind with the old ones?" Lone Eagle grinned.
"Bah."
"Ten is enough."
"Aiyee, many coup, many horses, and maybe a fat Crow woman for you, my brother."
"A child needs his sleep, so good night, my brother."

Wild Horse smiled then rolled into his buffalo robes and was asleep immediately. Lone Eagle sat and stared into the embers of the fire until late, trying to figure out what the whites wanted of him. Perhaps I have killed one of their people. No, I have not killed a white except for the one fighting with the Pawnee two summers ago. It was a fair fight; no, he did not think this the reason. What then, finally his eyes becoming heavy he rolled into his own blankets. Tall Bow studied his older son and shook his head. He, too, worried about the Look Alike One. Maybe he had strong medicine against Lone Eagle.

The sun boy in the east was barely visible when all the warriors who had left arrows gathered at the designated place outside the village. Pointing towards the south, Lone Eagle led the small group away from the village and towards the land of the Crow.

18

Press was ready, and Virginia had reluctantly pronounced him fit to ride. Finishing supper, Press motioned for Bill to follow him and they walked to where the horses were grazing.

"Tomorrow we look for the village of High Meadows."

"Which direction?"

"Don't know yet."

"Blind hunt again?"

"No, after dark I'll go see Lame Bull; maybe he'll point us in the right direction."

"Good luck, but I think we're on a wild goose chase."

"You're wrong, he's out there and I aim to find him."

Checking on the horses, making sure their hobbles were tight, the two men returned to the wagons where Press hunted up Raven and Crow Foot. "You have been with us long, my friends."

"Too long."

"Why have you stayed?"

"I have not paid the medicine woman back for giving me back my life."

"You do not owe her. She is a friend and friends help each other."

"I must pay her."

"Then help me find Lone Eagle. Do you know a chief named High Meadows?"

"I know of him."

"Could you find his village?"

"Yes, but it would be better if you asked Lame Bull. He has been to the village many times."

"I will council with Lame Bull later. If he will not help we will do the best we can, if you two will help."

"I will do this for you Tall One, and the Medicine Woman."

"Thank you, my friends." Press nodded to the two Cheyenne then walked towards the village of Lame Bull.

Virginia fell in beside him as he walked. Locking her arm in his, she pulled him to a stop. "Are you going to speak with Lame Bull?"

"Yes."

"Maybe I should go with you. The people are friendly towards me."

"No, an Indian village is no place for you after dark."

Kissing him, she stepped back and looked into his eyes."Press, be careful. If it comes to a choice, I want you safe; we'll leave Phillip behind."

"I'll find him, and I'll be careful. I owe it to the General to try."

Pulling her into his arms he kissed her passionately then released her. Looking at her in the darkening evening shadows, he knew she was the prettiest thing he had ever seen. Kissing her again, he turned her back towards the wagons. The sun was already down and the shadows were getting long beside the river when Press started to Lame Bull's village. A short fifteen minutes brought him to the edge of the camp. He had not been to Lame Bull's lodge but Raven had told him where it stood in the village. Reaching the lodge, he was about to announce his presence when a voice greeted him from the fire.

"Ishta Shakota is welcome to the lodge of Lame Bull," the aging chief said as he walked towards Press in the dark.

"Thank you, my uncle."

"Come, sit at the fire and eat with us."

Press was motioned to a seat by Lame Bull. An old squaw gave him a wooden bowl full of meat and wild onions. Not hungry, he still ate not wanting to offend his hosts.

"Thank you." Press spooned a mouthful of the stew into his mouth finding it was indeed tasty. Finishing the stew, he refused another thanking the old woman again. Muttering something about Press not eating enough to fill a papoose, she retreated into the lodge away from the men's talk. Lame Bull waited a sufficient time for good manners, then pulled out his pipe and offered it to Press, who pulled a mouthful of the acrid smoke into his mouth, then passed it back to Lame Bull.

"Why does the Mighty Heart come here after the sun sleeps?" One of the warriors around the fire questioned Press suspiciously.

"Does a friend have to come always in the daytime?" Press countered.

"Ishta Shakota is welcome in the village of the Sioux anytime." Lame Bull growled at the warrior making him pull back into the shadows of the fire.

"I have brought a present to my brothers." Press gestured around the circle of men. "A present the white men enjoy after a good meal." Press pulled out a bundle of the General's cigars from his coat pocket. Lighting one with an ember from the fire he blew smoke to the wind, making the warriors sniff the air. Passing them out he made sure to give the first one to the warrior who Lame Bull had rebuked. Press sat back and watched as every warrior lit his cigar. Trying to pretend he was enjoying his Press smiled, even though the thing was about to make him sick.

"Enjou, Mighty Heart, the little weed is better than the clay pipe." Lame Bull beamed.

Press could tell by the way the warriors were puffing on their cigars he had scored big with them. "I am glad my uncle likes them."

"Maybe not all things of the whites are bad." One of the warriors added.

After all the cigars were finished and the small talk amongst the warriors was at an end, Press figured it was a good time to make his bid for a guide.

"My uncle, I have other reasons for coming to the village of Lame Bull this night."

"Speak what is on your mind."

"As you know, I seek the warrior Lone Eagle. I know he belongs to the village of High Meadows and I come asking for a guide to take me there."

"Why do you wish to die?" A warrior asked.

"I do not seek death. I just wish to speak with Lone Eagle."

"To find him is to die." Another warrior spoke up.

"I do not believe this. I am a friend to all the Sioux. Have I not proven this?"

"He will kill you before you can prove you are a friend."

"I believe as great a leader as Lone Eagle is, he would not kill a friend no matter what color his skin is." Press argued.

"Why do you seek him?" Another voice questioned.

"You have seen the Look Alike One." Press did not hesitate. "You yourselves call him that because he looks like Lone Eagle, we just want them to meet."

"Bah! Not even a white would journey from the east just to meet a Sioux, not even the great Lone Eagle."

"I do not lie." Press spoke harshly at the insinuation he was lying.

"Ishta Shakota, my son." Lame Bull soothed the heated words before they became more. "No one says you lie; it's just that the Sioux do not understand why you seek Lone Eagle."

"I say he lies!" A large warrior leaped to his feet. "The whites come with the Look Alike One to make bad medicine against Lone Eagle."

"White Owl is a brave man. He knows the Mighty Heart one is still weak from his fight with the white trapper." Lame Bull rested his hand gently on Press' arm so he wouldn't rise to the challenge.

"If White Owl wants to fight tonight, he can fight Little Elk." The young warrior Lame Bull had rebuked earlier stepped in front of Press.

Sensing he was outnumbered, the warrior spat his contempt and left the fire. Press was shocked that Little Elk had stood up for him against a formidable foe like White Owl.

"I thank Little Elk." Press nodded at the young warrior.

"I shamed myself in front of my chief, and you, Ishta Shakota and I wished to save face." The warrior spoke then sat back down.

"I see no shame in a warrior who asks questions."

"In my Chief's lodge, I had no right."

"I see a young man brave and strong, who one day will be a great leader amongst his people." Press bragged on the warrior.

"Thank you, Ishta Shakota."

Lame Bull rose and motioned for Press to follow him inside his lodge. The rest of the warriors quietly retreated to their own lodges. Dismissing the old squaw, Lame Bull directed Press to sit and reached for his pipe.

"I have another of the little weeds, uncle."

"That would be good." Press handed the Chief the rest of the cigars and waited while he lighted one. Studying the small fire, the Chief puffed on the cigar several times, then cleared his throat.

"My son, before the time of the white traders, my village was the mightiest nation amongst the Sioux. The buffalo gave us food and clothing, everything we needed. The mother earth gave us our medicines and herbs, and the great Waken Taken gave us sons and daughters to keep the Sioux people strong and mighty. The whites with their guns and greed have taken away our power over the Crow, Pawnee, and Snakes. In my medicine dreams I have seen the many villages of the whites. My medicine shows me a war will come someday with the whites, and as great a nation as we are we will be no more. Maybe I am a tame Indian, but as long as I am Chief of my village I will stay at peace with the whites. My vision shows me it is the only way my people can survive the white man's flood. If all whites were as you and the medicine woman it would be different, but they are not. You have proven to be of good heart towards my people. You have come in search of Lone Eagle, there is no need to tell me the real reason you seek him; I know. I tell you these things because you are as I would wish my sons to be if they still walked the earth. I have known Lone Eagle since he first came to the Sioux and Tall Bow. He will be a great leader, the Sioux need him. No one in the Sioux Nation would betray him. You have asked me to lead you to him, this I cannot do, even for you. Anything else I would do. But I say this, leave this place, go back to the eastern lands. I have seen bad omens in the sky, and I fear for all of you. Leave this place while you can."

Lame Bull abruptly stopped and Press knew the subject was closed. Finding Lone Eagle would be up to Raven and Crow Foot now.

"I thank Lame Bull for his words, but we have journeyed far and we will not leave until we have found that which we seek." Press studied the effects his words would have on the old Chief.

"Then, I wish you much luck, my son."

Knowing their talk was at an end Press stood and left the lodge. Turning from the lodge, Press was about to walk away when he sensed another's presence in the dark.

"It is I, Little Elk."

"Little Elk!" Press was relieved, thinking maybe it was White Owl, knowing he was still too weak to fight.

"Lame Bull will not lead you to High Meadow's village." It was more of a statement than a question.

"No."

"It is as I thought."

"Lame Bull is the leader of his people. He must do what he thinks best for them."

"What will Ishta Shakota do now?"

"I will try to find the village of High Meadows."

"Alone?"

"I will take the Look Alike One and the two Cheyenne's."

"It is near the meat taking time. High Meadows will move his village closer to the buffalo grounds."

"Then we will look for him there."

"Many tribes look for the buffalo now; it will be very dangerous."

Press nodded in agreement. "We must try."

"Perhaps you will take Little Elk for a guide."

"What would Lame Bull say of this?"

"Each Sioux warrior does as his medicine tells him. No other can tell him what to do, not even Lame Bull."

"Then it would please me if Little Elk would lead us." Press held out his hand to the young warrior.

"Good; I will tell Lame Bull that I go."

"We will leave when the sun rises."

"I will meet you near the river at the talking rocks."

Waving his hand, Press walked back to the fort. When he arrived he was surprised to find everyone gathered around the fire waiting anxiously. Taking a cup of coffee from Elizabeth, Press sat next to Virginia and explained what had happened. "I have found us a guide."

"Hallelujah." Horatio slapped his leg and smiled.

"We must be ready to leave at dawn. We'll need a packhorse with trade goods and supplies for at least a week."

"An offering, for the heathens?" Bill questioned.

"No Bill; a goodwill offering, if we get close enough to use them." Press answered.

"Will there be danger?" Elizabeth asked.

Press looked at Virginia. "There's always danger out here."

"I will be ready at dawn." Horatio stood up.

"No, Sir; it would be better if you stayed and looked after Virginia and Elizabeth." Press braced himself for the upcoming argument, but to his surprise Horatio agreed.

"You're right of course."

"I will speak with Raven and Crow Foot; they will watch over them too."

"Let me take a look at your side before you go to bed." Virginia motioned Press closer to the fire. "It looks fine, but I don't want you overdoing it."

"Yes, Doctor." Press smiled.

"And be careful."

"Yes, Doctor."

"Press, it's not funny, if I should lose you...." She turned her face.

Cupping his hand around her chin he smiled down at her. "Nothing's going to happen; besides, I'll have your big brother to protect me."

"I love you, Preston Forbes." Virginia kissed him, then hurried to the wagon leaving Press alone with a warm feeling in his chest.

Walking to where Raven and Crow Foot sat around their small fire, Press quickly told them what had happened and his plans for leaving, asking that they see after Horatio and the women in his absence.

"It is good that you have found someone to lead you. I will stay and guard the medicine woman with my life." Raven spoke solemnly.

"Thank you, that's all a friend could ask of another friend."

"When you return, it will be time for us to return to our people." Crow Foot added.

"I would someday like to travel to your village, and see the great Cheyenne people.

"The Cheyenne would be proud to have Ishta Shakota amongst us." Nodding his head, Press walked to his blankets and rolled into them. Looking above him at the brilliant stars that were shining he wondered how Lone Eagle would indeed greet them.

True to his word Little Elk was waiting at the rapids, the place the Sioux called the Talking Rocks. Press noticed the young warrior was heavily armed with all the articles of war a Sioux warrior normally carried on the war trail. Not a word was spoken as they rode up to him; Little Elk just turned his horse and started across the river.

All day they pushed the horses hard, stopping only occasionally to study the far horizon for riders. Twice riders were seen in the distance but too far away to tell what tribe they were. At dark Little Elk pulled into a stand of willows near a small stream and dismounted.

Press stepped down from his horse, only nodding when Bill questioned if he was alright. "I'll take care of the horses. Find you a soft spot and light." Bill volunteered.

"Thanks, this time I'm going to let you do it." Press pulled his saddlebags from the sorrel and handed Bill the reins. Little Elk was already piling a few leaves together for his night's bed. Pulling out biscuits and hardtack, Press offered the warrior some, but Little Elk politely refused, showing Press his bag of jerked meat.

"Where's the coffee?" Bill asked, coming in after hobbling the horses.

"No coffee, cold camp."

"That's un American."

"Tell Little Elk that; he's running this show."

"I would, but I doubt he'd understand me."

Daylight found the three traveling south, two hours from the dry camp where they had spent the night. Bill was still haranguing Press for not having his morning coffee.

"I promise you, as soon as we can light a fire I'm going to make you a whole pot of the blackest, hottest coffee you can drink."

"White eyes talk too much. Maybe enemy come take out tongue." Little Elk hissed from where he rode. Press looked to where the warrior sat his horse and nodded. Motioning for Bill to be quiet, Press berated himself for having to be told to be quiet. After spending all those miles with Monk, he should have known better.

Following Little Elk through a natural pass, they were almost halfway across a large valley, when the warrior reined his horse in violently, causing Press to bump him. Dismounting quickly, Little Elk put his ear to the ground. Swinging back on his horse, he motioned for Bill and Press to follow. Whipping his horse into a hard run, he retraced their steps back up the valley. Suddenly the valley floor started shaking as hundreds of stampeding buffalo came pouring down the valley behind the fleeing horsemen.

The horses were running full out, their necks stretched to the limit. Not having to be urged on, now they ran in sheer fright from the roar and danger that followed. Suddenly, Press watched as Bill's horse stumbled in a hole and fell, sending Bill catapulting over his head. Press fought his horse, pulling the frightened animal to a halt, then riding back to where Bill had fallen.

Seeing the futility of lifting Bill's unconscious body across the saddle of his plunging horse, Press turned the gelding loose and started dragging Bill towards a pile of rocks.

Straining with all his remaining strength, Press just managed to pull the big man behind a huge boulder, when the herd was upon them. The dust was so thick from the passing herd Press thought he might pass out from lack of oxygen. Shrugging out of his coat, Press covered Bill's face hoping to keep out all the dust particles he could. The stench from the herd was almost as bad as the dust. Press hoped Bill wouldn't come to and lunge to his feet. He knew he didn't have the strength left to hold him down.

Minutes passed, seeming like hours, before the last of the herd passed, leaving the two men buried in dirt clods thrown up by the running buffalo. Pulling the coat from Bill's face Press was amazed when his friend looked at him and grinned. "You're awake!"

"Well, I ain't dead."

"I was afraid you'd wake up and try to get up."

"In the middle of a buffalo stampede!"

"I didn't figure you knew what was going on."

"Sure I knew; we have them all the time back in Philadelphia." Bill laughed.

"Can't you be serious for once?" Press shook his head.

"Sure can. Guess you better know I've got a broke leg."

Press looked at Bill's left leg, and he knew, as it protruded out at an ugly angle. Running his hand over the leg, Press felt where the break was. "It's broke sure enough."

"No kidding, I'd appreciate it if you'd keep your hands off of it." Bill groaned.

"Sorry, just checking."

"Take my word, it's broke all right."

"Well, you picked a good time to break it."

"Peers to me, if you've got to break a leg, one time is as good as another."

"Funny man, sure wish your sister was here."

"What for?"

"I'm going to have to set it."

"True enough, what do you need her for?"

"To sit on you. You big lunkhead." Press slapped at Bill's bare head. "I guess it could be worse."

"Sure could, for one thing that Indian bringing our horses in could be hostile."

"Little Elk." Press leaped to his feet waving. The young warrior rode up to the two men, smiling broadly. He really hadn't expected to find the two white men alive. Too many times he had seen men trampled under the rampaging stampede of a buffalo run.

"Ishta Shakota, it's good you are alive."

"It is good to be alive."

"The Look Alike One is hurt?"

"Broken leg."

"I will get willow shoots from the river, we will fix leg good." The young Sioux turned his horse, loping off towards the end of the valley.

Several minutes passed, and Little Elk returned with a bundle of dried willow branches. Stretching Bill out, Press cut the britches leg out of his pants then studied the leg. The bone had not broken through the skin.

"Bill, this is going to hurt and I don't have the strength left to hold you." Press started to say something else when Bill interrupted.

"Set it, I'll be still."

"I will do it." Little Elk motioned for Press to hold Bill's upper leg as best he could.

"Handy fellow." Bill grunted as the bone grated back into place. Placing the willow branches around the leg, the Sioux secured them with leather thongs cut from Bill's britches.

Studying his work Little Elk nodded, then mounted his horse. Minutes passed before he was back with several larger poles. "Travois."

"He cannot travel!" Press argued as the young warrior started lashing the poles together.

"It is better to travel sick and live, than to die in this place."

"Do you see trouble, my friend?"

"One must always see trouble in a strange place."

"What's all the arguing about?" Bill asked, sweat pouring from his face.

"Little Elk says we need to go, now."

"Let's go, I'll ride in style."

"It's your leg."

Cushioning the travois with several trade blankets, it took both Little Elk and Press to lift the heavy man onto the travois. Covering Bill then wrapping a rope around him to keep the bouncing of the travois from jarring him off, Press looked down at his work. "We're ready."

Little Elk led off to the north with Press leading the travois horse. Press had thought about taking Bill back to Fort Laramie, but Bill insisted that they continue. Little Elk assured them the medicine man of the Ogallalas could mend Bill's leg when they reached the village. They had traveled several miles when Little Elk stopped on a high bluff and looked over a valley they were skirting. Raising his arm he pointed a finger.

"Ogallala Sioux."

"How far?"

"You wait here; I go find; tell people who we are, maybe there will be no trouble." Little Elk dropped the lead rope of the pack horse. "You bring Look Alike One slow."

"Good, we will follow slow."

"Enjou." Little Elk headed in the direction of the village, then turned his horse. "If I no come back, you go quick and be ready with fire stick."

An hour had passed when Press spotted riders coming at a slow lope. It was still too far to tell if Little Elk was with them. Press slid from his horse and checked the priming of their weapons, then slid Bill's rifle under the blankets with him.

The group of warriors, with Little Elk in front, came in at a slow trot, and stopped a few feet from where Press and Bill waited. "My brothers!" Little Elk turned to look at the warriors behind him. "This is the great warrior Ishta Shakota, the one that killed the evil white trapper Larouche, when he attacked Lame Bull. He is a friend to the Sioux."

A dignified warrior, sitting his prancing horse, proudly rode up to Press and gave him the friendship sign. "I have heard of your courage, you are welcome in the village of the people."

"And I have heard much of the great Ogallala People and their Chief High Meadows." Press returned the sign.

Looking down at Bill, the older warrior nodded several times. "This is the Look Alike One we have heard about."

"Yes, his real name is Bill."

"Bill!" the warrior tried to pronounce the word. "The Look Alike One is better."

"It is a fitting name." Press agreed.

"Come, we go village."

19

With the warrior leading and the Sioux warriors surrounding the travois, the party descended into a large valley dotted heavily with trees. A deep creek ran the course of the meadows, and Press could see from a military man's view point that the village would be easily defended against an enemy. Riders coming down into the valley would be quickly detected in time to give the alarm. A large horse herd guarded by younger boys grazed contentedly on the deep summer grass.

Smoke from the numerous campfires drifted lazily into the afternoon sky. Nearing the village, Press estimated over one hundred lodges made up the village. Mentally calculating he figured at least a hundred and fifty full grown warriors could be with High Meadows. The entire village was on hand to watch the newcomers and to see the Look Alike One, and the one with the Mighty Heart they had heard so much about. Tall Bow stopped the riders in front of a large lodge near the center of the village. Setting his horse quietly he waited until a gray haired elder stepped into view.

"Greetings, Blue Thunder." The warrior dismounted easily from his horse.

"Greetings, Tall Bow."

"We have visitors."

"Yes, I have seen them coming in my dreams."

"One is hurt."

"Yes, the Look Alike One has a broken leg." This time Press was bewildered. How did the old man know Bill was the one hurt? Perhaps Little Elk had said something.

"He needs your medicine."

The old one's eyes settled on Press and remained there, quietly looking into his blue eyes. Press was surprised at the strange sadness on the man's face. "You are Ishta Shakota, the mighty heart who helped Lame Bull against the white trappers!"

"Yes."

"I am Blue Thunder, medicine man of the Ogallala, and for what you have done and for what the Medicine Woman has done, I will help the Look Alike One; bring him into my lodge."

Bill was placed on a buffalo hide bed where the medicine man quickly removed the splint and studied Bill's leg. Probing gently on the leg he nodded then washed the broken place with some kind of herbal solution before again applying a splint.

"The leg will heal quickly; he is as strong as a horse." Blue Thunder predicted as he finished with Bill.

"Thank you, Blue Thunder."

"No, my son, it is I who thanks you."

"Why is that?"

"Many, many moons ago, when I was a young warrior, I had a vision of a tall warrior coming into our village. This one also had a broken leg and he looked the same as another. My vision was long ago. I thought maybe the great ones above had forgotten, but I see now they have not."

"Was there more in your vision?" Press was truly curious.

"Yes, but we will speak of that later." The old one shrugged his shoulders.

"I have heard that Blue Thunder was the greatest of all medicine men. Now I see these words are true." Press bragged on Blue Thunder, watching his words take effect, and in truth, he believed there was something special about this man.

"I have been Shaman of my people many summers, more than I can remember. There have been good times, plenty to eat, much happiness. There have also been hungry times when the buffalo do not come and the people hunger. This is to be endured. But, now I see another time coming, a bad time for my people. I see much sadness, much death. I would speak with you later of this, but now High Meadows waits for you."

Following Blue Thunder outside, Press walked with him towards a large lodge where several older warriors sat stoically in front of it. Blue Thunder motioned for a place for Press to sit then took his own place. "My Chief,

High Meadows." Blue Thunder acknowledged the warrior beside him as he sat down.

Press had been wrong this was not the warrior who had brought them in from the pass. This one almost looked the same but had a more proud aura about him, if that was possible.

"You are welcome to my lodge, Ishta Shakota." Press nodded then watched as the ceremonial pipe was produced. Looking around the circle his eyes stopped on the warrior he had thought was High Meadows earlier. They looked almost identical except the Chief seemed older.

"He is Tall Bow, brother of our Chief and father of Lone Eagle," Blue Thunder whispered seeing Press looking at the two men.

When the pipe had been passed, High Meadows rose slowly to his feet and addressed the assembled warriors for several minutes. Reminding them of the past injustices of the whites, then telling them of all the good things the medicine woman and Ishta Shakota had done for the people.

"You and the Look Alike One are welcome in the village of the Ogallala People." High Meadows sat back down and looked to where Press sat.

"Thank you, great Chief." Press had stood knowing it was his turn to speak. "And, I thank Blue Thunder for fixing the leg of the Look Alike One. Also I thank Little Elk for bringing us to this place where we can talk." Press nodded to where Little Elk stood outside the circle of elders. "We have brought gifts for the people, not to trade for buffalo robes, not for beaver pelts, or the fast ponies of the Sioux. No my friends, we've brought these gifts as presents to our friends the Sioux People."

"Ishta Shakota speaks good words, and brags on the Sioux, but does he speak the truth and respect us as his words say?" A warrior spoke from the circle.

"I have much respect for the Sioux."

"It is said you are a soldier at the pony fort." Another spoke up.

"This is true."

"We too, remember the treaty day and you were a soldier there that day." High Meadows spoke this time.

"I was there at the treaty, but now I'm not in the army."

"Did the white man's army send you to us?"

"No, I am here because of the Look Alike One and his father."

"Why?" another asked.

"My friends, my children," Blue Thunder stood, raising his arms to quieten the warriors before they became quarrelsome towards Press. "Ishta Shakota is here because of me. I brought the Look Alike One to us so my vision of long ago could be fulfilled. They are not spies or enemies, they are friends, and it is my wish that you cool your tongues and greet them as friends, for I truly believe they are indeed the friends of our people."

Words this strong from the mouth of Blue Thunder could not be unheeded. The uproar that was coming diminished and all shook their heads in agreement.

"Then tell us my son, why have you and the Look Alike One come into our lands?" High Meadows asked politely.

Studying the faces gathered around him Press remembered how Monk had told him an Indian loved a good story almost as much as a good horse. Telling the story of General Lane, of his greatness in battle, of the Lane family, and the disappearance of Phillip, Press watched as the interest grew in the faces of the warriors. Especially about the General, his great army, and battles. He added lastly that the general didn't wish to take Lone Eagle from them he just wanted to see his lost grandson before he died. Finished, he returned to his seat beside High Meadows.

"Is this General the one that plays with the children of Lame Bull's village?" A warrior asked.

"Yes."

"Could one who plays with children be so terrible in battle?"

"It is true, he plays with the children but I, Ishta Shakota, say to you, never has the Great Spirit made a war chief as terrible in battle as this one."

"Is he braver than the Sioux?"

"He is as brave."

"Has he counted many coup?"

"He has captured as many enemy in a day as the Sioux have horses." Most of the warriors wagged their heads in disbelief causing Press to think he had bragged too much.

"Ishta Shakota, these words are easy to say, but hard to prove."

"I do not lie; my word is my proof."

"I have seen this great warrior in my visions slaying enemies, making them fall like leaves from a tree. Ishta Shakota does not lie." Blue Thunder spoke up.

Press could not tell if the wily old medicine man was trying to help him or strengthen his own powers over the people.

"Tell us more of the white man's warriors and fighting and about the big gun that throws fire and death with a loud boom." A younger warrior spoke, causing several heads to shake in agreement.

Press smiled; he knew the warrior was speaking of the cannon at the fort. Launching into a long oration about the cannon, Horatio and his armies, Press used fact, fiction, and some down right exaggeration to keep the warriors rapt attention until early morning.

The council ended with Press answering questions about the whites in the east, and the Medicine Woman. Press was surprised they knew of the necklace, and of her saving the lives of Raven, and of Malachi and his great fight with the bear. With a signal from High Meadows the warriors dispersed, leaving only the Chief and Blue Thunder seated with Press.

"You spoke well tonight, Ishta Shakota."

"Thank you my Chief, I spoke the truth from my heart."

"I would like to meet this great General someday."

"He wishes to come here to meet you."

"That is good. Now it is late, but there is one who would speak with you alone."

"Lone Eagle?" Press questioned. He had looked hard but the warrior had not been present at the council, nor had he seen him anywhere as they rode in.

"No, Lone Eagle is not here, he has ridden to the south, but my brother Tall Bow would like words with you."

"Yes, I would like to speak with Tall Bow."

"Good, his lodge is there." High Meadows pointed out the lodge of his brother.

Press spoke to Blue Thunder as he turned to leave. "I will come to see the Look Alike One in the morning."

Press walked to the lodge of Tall Bow and asked permission to enter. Stepping into the lodge he found himself looking across a small fire at the father of the man he had come so far to find. Press waited until the warrior motioned to a place in front of him to sit. This was the first time he hadn't been asked to sit on his host's left; maybe he wasn't so honored in this lodge.

"Welcome to my lodge, Ishta Shakota. I thank you for coming." The warrior spoke quietly. Press looked at the man and knew he wasn't being disrespectful, but wanted to look into his face as they spoke.

"I thank you for inviting me to talk." For some reason Press respected this warrior even though they had just met; something, maybe his quiet manner and honest face.

"It is not often that a white respects the people."

"Cannot a man have a good heart towards all people?"

"Yes, but it has never been so. I asked you to my lodge so we can speak alone away from other's ears."

"This is as I wish it too."

"You speak our language well."

Press related his teachings from Monk and their trip west.

"Yes, I know this one; he wintered with us on the Yellowstone, a long time ago." Tall Bow nodded.

"He said this, too."

"He is a good man, but I don't believe his heart is truly for the red man."

"He is a hard man, but a good man."

"Tell me of the Look Alike One."

Press started from the beginning, telling Tall Bow from the first time he had met Bill until their arrival in the village. At the story of the killing of the white horse thieves Tall Bow became more alert and jumped into the conversation.

"Why did you not wish to kill the ones that stole your horses?"

"There was no need."

"A Sioux always kills his enemies."

"Always?" Press countered.

"Sometimes we take them as slaves to be adopted into the tribe if they are willing."

"Then, we think the same. You do not always kill."

"Yet, you killed the evil trapper!"

"Yes."

"Because of an Indian?"

"Yes."

"The Look Alike One, is he of good heart?"

"He is of a different heart. He belongs back east in the white man's world."

"But he killed the white pony stealers."

"Yes."

"Does he enjoy killing?"

Press stared thoughtfully into the fire, his thoughts returning to different times he had seen Bill in fights. Tall Bow studied his face as he thought back. "This I do not know."

"He is your friend, is he not?"

"We are as brothers."

"Yet, you do not know his heart."

"No."

"Is he a brave man?"

"None are as brave or as fierce in a fight."

"My other son, Wild Horse, says Lone Eagle and the Look Alike One are as alike as two twin buffalo calves."

"This is so."

"You have seen Lone Eagle?"

"Yes, at the Laramie Treaty council."

This time it was Tall Bow who stared for several minutes into the fire. "I have seen this coming many times in my dreams."

"Why does the Look Alike One bother you? We mean no harm to Lone Eagle, nor would we take him from this place even if we could." Press reassured Tall Bow.

"It is not you I fear, but Lone Eagle."

"Why?"

"My son's heart is bad against the whites. He has seen many bad things happen to the people. His mother was killed, when he was small, by Indians led by a white. I do not wish to see him fight against his own brother."

"Then you know they are brothers?"

"Yes."

"Lone Eagle is not of your blood then?"

"No, he is not of my blood, but I have given him the heart of the people and I love him as much, maybe even more. Tell me of the medicine woman."

He smiled remembering back to the first time he had seen the freckled faced spindly girl who reminded him so much of a frisky young colt bouncing across a green meadow. "She is hard to tell about without bragging."

"Is it not strange, even in a white mans world for her to be a medicine woman?"

"Yes, at first, but the people have come to trust her; she is truly incredible."

"Raven would give his life for her."

"We all would."

"Be careful my son, Raven might steal her." These words caused both men to laugh.

"Tell me uncle, would it be possible for Lone Eagle to meet with the old one so that he might see his grandson before he goes to meet the Great Spirits?"

"We will see, I will ask him when he returns; I will speak strongly for it."

"I thank you; that is all I can ask."

"I would like for you to bring the old one and the medicine woman here. I would like to see this great warrior and his beautiful daughter." Tall Bow was truly intrigued. "When you go for them I will send warriors to protect them."

"I would have to leave the Look Alike One here. He will be unable to travel for awhile."

"He will be protected; you have my word. No one will harm him and he is welcome." Press felt like Tall Bow was speaking of Lone Eagle, should he return.

"I will talk to the Look Alike One when he awakes."

Bill was asleep when Press returned to Blue Thunder's lodge, but Little Elk was wide awake and anxious to hear everything that had been said.

"I thought you Indians were supposed to be stoic?" Press grinned as Little Elk popped questions at him.

"Ah, my brother, you forget I am a tame Indian."

"I doubt that very much, but if you are, heaven help me if I meet a wild one."

"Now, what was said?"

"Tomorrow little brother, tonight I am tired."

Press hadn't realized he had spoken with Tall Bow so long into the night. Following Little Elk to the lodge that had been prepared for them, he fell into his robes and was asleep before his head hit the ground.

20

At Horatio's insistence Virginia and Elizabeth had stayed close to the fort since Bill and Press had left for High Meadow's village. After two days, boredom had set in and the two girls, catching Horatio away from the wagon, had wandered down to the river. Talking and laughing the two young women were not aware of the approaching danger crossing the river above them. The late summer day was beautiful with the birds singing and squirrels scolding them from the tree tops. Hearing the heavy beat of running horses the girls looked up to see a band of riders hideously painted, thundering towards them. Too late to run, the girls stood frozen as the horses plunged to a stop encircling them.

Staring defiantly at the warriors, they tried to run through the horses, but were caught in vise like holds, and held powerless in the hands of the stronger warriors. Virginia dropped her medical bag that she had brought along intending to check on the sick ones in the nearby village. A warrior snatched the bag from the ground and tossed it to one of the other riders.

A guttural command from the leader, and the girls were drug across the withers in front of two warriors and the war party raced back towards the river. Virginia knew these were not Sioux, but she didn't know what tribe they were from. Elizabeth struggled valiantly trying to escape, but a hard cuff to the head quieted her.

Holding the medallion out to who seemed like the leader, she gasped when he wrenched it from her neck and hurled it to the ground. Whipping their horses into a hard lope, they traveled fast, putting distance between the fort and themselves, stopping from time to time only long enough to blow their horses. At one stop Virginia spoke encouragement to Elizabeth only to receive a hard cuff herself. Darkness found the raiders far from the fort. Virginia and Elizabeth were exhausted, not used to riding bareback and at such a pace. Halting in a tangle of cedars and underbrush the warriors dismounted and pulled the girls to the ground. Tying them to small trees they left one hand loose, then tossed some dried jerky at their feet and walked off.

Elizabeth hurled the meat at one of the warriors, hitting him in the back. The warrior laughed and made an obscene gesture at his loin cloth and then at the girls. Elizabeth spit in his direction and picked up a small rock which made the man laugh again. A word from the leader and the men returned to their jerky, completely ignoring the women.

"You need to eat." Virginia offered Elizabeth a piece of her jerky.

"I'm not hungry."

"I think they are Crows, enemies of the Sioux and Cheyenne."

"I think they are a lot worse than that."

"It would help if you'd calm down a little."

"Calm down!" Elizabeth scowled.

"We've gotten ourselves into a fix here, now we need to stay calm and think."

"Okay, okay."

"If they are Crows, they are a long way into enemy territory."

"Is that good?"

"By now Grandfather knows we are gone and is probably following."

"I wish Press or Mr. Monk were at the fort."

Virginia thought it funny Elizabeth hadn't mentioned Bill, only Monk and Press. "Don't worry, Crow Foot and Raven will be following."

"If one of those heathens touch me I'll cut out his liver, even if he kills me."

"They don't seem to have that on their minds."

"I've heard that's what they do to white women captives."

"Hopefully, these men are different."

"They are men, aren't they?"

After a couple of hours rest for the horses, the girls were kicked roughly awake and slung on horses. Virginia had to hand it to Elizabeth, she put up another good fight and received another good slap. Slinging Elizabeth belly down across a horse, the man gave her a good wallop across her backside that caused her to lash out at him in fury.

"Elizabeth, stop it."

The leader of the raiders looked sharply at Virginia then motioned towards the northwest. Mid afternoon found them along a beautiful river where the girls were allowed a few minutes alone.

"We can escape, they are out of sight."

"Escape where and outrun horses? Next time they won't let you out of their sight, and I don't think you'll like that."

A warrior came to where they were talking and roughly shoved Elizabeth towards the horses. Pushing him back she received another sound slap that sent her reeling on the rocky bank of the river. Coming up with a large rock she let fly with it catching the warrior alongside the head sending him backwards into the river. Sputtering and wet, the warrior came out of the water, his skinning knife pointed at Elizabeth. The laughter and ridicule from the other warriors only seemed to infuriate the warrior more as he advanced towards Elizabeth. Stepping between Elizabeth and the warrior, Virginia stood there, waiting as the man advanced. A sharp command from the leader stopped the warrior in his tracks. Stepping beside Virginia, he spoke sharply to the warriors then nodded at Virginia. Elizabeth's face had started bruising from the hard slaps she had received, but Virginia knew that they had been lucky so far.

Virginia had to admit Elizabeth was giving back as good as she got. Several of the warriors had bruises on them from the rocks Elizabeth could get her hands on. Virginia had been afraid that the warriors would tire of fighting with her, but to the contrary, they seemed to enjoy the conflict with the dark haired woman with the evil temper. The pace had slowed after three hard days of riding and Virginia figured they were getting closer to their own lands.

"I think we may be getting close to their village." Virginia commented when the raiders stopped for the night.

"Good."

"Why is that good, Elizabeth?"

"I've got a few words to say to their wives."

"Elizabeth." Virginia was exasperated. "I don't think these men will care what you say to their wives, if they have wives."

"We'll see about that." Elizabeth stuck out her chin.

Virginia tensed as the leader approached where the girls were sitting. She stared evenly into the dark face of the man. A broad forehead, hooked nose and wide lips gave him an evil look, but something in the man's manner convinced Virginia he meant no harm to her or Elizabeth. Speaking to Virginia, the man shook his massive head when Virginia could not understand him. Turning to leave he stopped and turned back, and in broken syllables tried another language.

"That's French." Elizabeth exclaimed.

"You sure? I can't understand anything he's saying."

"It's French alright, rough, but it's what he's trying to speak. Wonder where he learned French?"

"Who cares? For pete's sake. What's he saying?"

"I think he's calling you medicine something or other."

"Tell him sometimes I am called that."

"He wants to know if that is your medicine." Elizabeth pointed to Virginia's medical bag.

"Tell him it is."

"Now, he wants to know if you have great powers."

"Tell him I can cure people, sometimes."

"He wants to know if you can make the evil ones leave the belly of a sick one?"

"Ask him where the pain is."

"He says belly hot here." Elizabeth pointed to her side.

"Appendicitis, ask him where the sick one is."

"He says, one more days ride."

"Ask him how he knew of me?"

Virginia listened as Elizabeth and the warrior conversed for several minutes. "His name is Yellow Moon of the Crow People. He says all of the people of the plains have heard of the Medicine Woman and her magic. He says the Cheyenne dogs have passed the word on, and he knows you are the adopted daughter of his sworn enemy Two Dogs."

"Ask him how long the man has had the evil ones in his stomach."

"Gin, you're starting to talk like these heathens."

"Well, you know what they say, When in Rome …!"

"I know, do as the Romans do."

"Ask him."

"He says several days."

"Tell him if we are to save the sick one, we must hurry."

"He says we go now."

"Tell him one more thing. When we finish, whether the man lives or dies I want his word he will take us back to the fort."

"He says maybe, him see."

"No, tell him I want his word now or I will do nothing."

Yellow Moon studied the face of the defiant red head and shook his head in agreement. "He wants to know if all white women are as mean as we are."

"Must be someone important to him."

"It is his adopted father, a white man."

"Let's hope he is still alive."

"You know, when you get past the nose, he is some man." Elizabeth studied the back of the man as he walked off.

"Elizabeth Hudson!"

"It doesn't hurt to look."

"I don't know what to think of you sometimes. One of these days your flirting is going to get you into trouble."

21

Lone Eagle and his warriors had traveled steadily for several days to the west. Crossing the Snake River, Lone Eagle placed scouts out and slowed his horses to a walk.

"We are getting near the Crow Villages." A warrior whispered quietly to Lone Eagle.

"Yes, Grey Badger, their villages will not be far from the river this late in the meat taking time."

"There." The warrior pointed towards a far hill.

"Smoke." Lone Eagle nodded.

"And Crow buffalo ponies under the smoke."

Raiding into the Crow hunting grounds was dangerous and sometimes very foolhardy, but to steal horses from the great Yellow Moon and his white father would be the greatest honor. Far into enemy territory they would be pursued, as there was no way to keep the stealing of horses a secret. Sending Grey Badger ahead alone, Lone Eagle held the rest of his raiding party in a stand of maples along the river. Two hours passed before Grey Badger made his way back silently to the group of anxious warriors.

"It is good."

"You have seen the village, my friend?" Lone Eagle questioned.

"Yes, Lone Eagle." The warrior drew in the soft sand. "The horses are here, the village sets like this. We can escape to the south without going into the village."

"Guards?"

"Only one, the Crow dogs feel safe so far into their hunting grounds."

"There should be more guards on the herd." Lone Eagle was suspicious.

"Aiyee, the great spirit gives us the horses." Another warrior spoke up.

"The village is very large, many warriors." Grey Badger continued. "Someone has died, the women darken their faces."

"The village of Yellow Moon would be large."

"If it is Yellow Moon's village he would have more guards out." Lone Eagle argued.

"The great ones have put the Crow ponies in our hands. Let us take them now." Big Bull spoke up.

"No, something is not right here; we will leave our ponies with one man, then move closer to the herd."

With Grey Badger leading, the warriors moved out afoot in single file. An hour slipped by before Grey Badger stopped at the edge of a large meadow where the horses grazed peacefully. "Wild Horse, go that way and check for guards. Tall Bear, that way." Lone Eagle slipped back into the cover of the trees so the herd wouldn't smell them and give the alarm.

The moon rose slowly while the warriors waited for their scouts. "Soon the bright one will light the whole meadow, my brother." Grey Badger whispered beside Lone Eagle.

Something is wrong here. Yellow Moon is too wily to leave his horse herd unprotected, Lone Eagle thought to himself. Perhaps it is a trap, but how would the Crow Chief know they were coming. Unless, a hunter could have spotted them?

"I think Yellow Moon has been warned."

"No, he has grown old and lazy and lay's with his squaws; he suspicions nothing." Grey Badger replied.

"We will wait for Wild Horse to return."

Lone Eagle had not gained his respect as a leader by acting foolhardy or reckless. To lose horses was one thing but to lose men would mean to lose face. Tall Bow had always taught his sons patience, and many times waiting had paid off for Lone Eagle. He would not be tempted to hurry into disaster by his eager warriors.

A slight blur in the dark and Wild Horse appeared silently beside his brother. "It is good, Lone Eagle, one guard only, and now he sleeps with his ancestors." Wild Horse held up the topknot of a Crow warrior.

"We go. Take the best horses quickly and return here."

Grey Badger fingered the braided ropes he carried and mumbled. "Yes, very quickly!"

"Is the great warrior, Grey Badger, afraid of a few Crows?" Wild Horse teased.

"My young friend, I am not great. There are many Crows and yes, I am afraid. I would not like for my body to be cut into little pieces by their squaws." Grey Badger smiled in the moonlight.

Wild Horse laughed easily. "Grey Badger is the bravest warrior I know, and he fears nothing."

Grey Badger was one of Lone Eagles most trusted and closest friends, and Wild Horse knew he did know the meaning of fear. The warriors slipped quietly into the Crow pony herd, each man searching out the beautiful and swift buffalo ponies. Long of leg and deep of chest they were easily spotted even in the dark of the moon. Trained not to leave a warrior's side they were easily roped and led away to where one warrior waited to hold them for the rest of the warriors. The Crow's buffalo ponies were the greatest prize, outside of personal bravery, that a man desired. In the meat taking time a good buffalo runner was worth several horses. And the Crow People had the best.

Lone Eagle passed up several horses in search of the one he had spotted as he entered the herd. If he was not mistaken the great gray stallion with the black legs was the one Yellow Moon was riding when they fought on the Musselshell two summers ago. The speed of the great horse had kept Lone Eagle from victory that day. Never, except for his Nez Perce stallion, had he seen a horse move as fast and as quick as the gray.

To capture the horse and bring him back to the people would be the biggest insult he could give to Yellow Moon and his white father, who was called Gordon. Moving silently, he spotted the stallion grazing quietly alone. Lone Eagle was surprised Yellow Moon would leave the horse unprotected with the herd. The stallion raised his head pointing his small ears as the strange smell of Lone Eagle approached. "Come great one. We will run the buffalo together and let the wind blow our faces as we race across the prairies." Lone Eagle crooned quietly to the stud.

Stepping closer, a quick flick of the wrist and the rawhide rope settled easily around the great neck. Startled, the stud backed up, but his training took over, he knew the rope would bite deeply if he fought.

"That is good, my friend." Lone Eagle talked softly as he took the slack from his rope. "You will be a present to my father, Tall Bow; you will make him proud."

Quickly making a halter of the rope, Lone Eagle swung easily upon the broad back. Snaring one more leggy bay gelding, he rode back to where the warriors were assembling.

"Aiyee, my brother, I know this one. He is the same horse the Crow Chief was riding when we fought with them two summers ago."

"Yes, my brother, the same. He will be a gift to our father."

"He is indeed a great one." Grey Badger grinned. "You have taken a great prize."

"All of you have too." Lone Eagle said looking around at all the horses the warriors were holding.

"Tonight the great spirit was with us." A warrior spoke up.

"Let us go before the Crows are with us too." Grey Badger spoke.

"We go." Lone Eagle led off in the direction the horse holder waited.

Daylight was near as they re-crossed the river and headed towards their own hunting grounds. The raiders had presented the horse holder with two sorrel buffalo runners when they stopped to water the horses. "They are beauties; thank you my friends." White Antelope ran his hand over the horses.

"We go, ride the horses we came here on if the Crows follow we will have fresh horses." Lone Eagle ordered.

Leading the way east at a fast trot, Lone Eagle arrived back at the big river at noon. Sliding to the ground in a stand of poplar trees, he waited for the rest of the warriors to dismount. "Grey Badger will lead the warriors toward our lands." Lone Eagle spoke to the warrior.

"And you?"

"I will talk with Wild Horse then rejoin you quickly."

"Hoka Hey, we go." Grey badger mounted and led the warriors away.

"The warriors will go ahead," said Lone Eagle placing his great hand on Wild Horse's shoulder. "You will wait here to see if the Crows follow."

"It is a great honor, I will wait."

"Watch till the sun is high above, then return to us."

White Horse nodded his head swelling with pride. Lone Eagle had given him much responsibility today. "I will follow you when the sun is high."

"Be careful Wild Horse. We make fun and joke about the Crows, but they are great warriors and this is their country."

"I will be careful."

"It was a good raid." Lone Eagle took the rope halters of the horses Wild Horse led.

"Yes, but we did not get you a fat Crow woman."

"Bah, am I too old to get my own woman?"

"Well, my brother, you are not as easy to look at as I am." Wild Horse grinned.

"Nor do I talk as much."

"Talking is an art Lone Eagle should learn if he is to become leader of the Sioux Nation."

"There is a time to talk; now is the time to act."

"Do not worry, I will return when the father sun goes behind the mountains to the west."

"This is good."

"Take good care of my ponies."

"As I would mine."

"This is what worries me, big brother; you might give them away."

Lone Eagle turned. Leading the horses he disappeared from Wild Horse' sight. Thinking of Walks Alone, he looked back one last time, then kicked his horse into a lope. He hadn't wanted to leave Wild Horse behind as a lookout, but as leader of the raider's he could not stay himself; and it would not look good to leave another. Grey Badger would have stayed, but it would not be fair to favor Wild Horse. Still he knew the wildness in the young warrior, the same wildness that was in Walks Alone; neither knew fear and both were reckless in battle.

"You have given Wild Horse much honor today." Grey Badger spoke as Lone Eagle caught up to them.

"Maybe too much honor!"

"Do not worry, my friend."

"Perhaps I should have left one of the older warriors behind."

"A man would of thought of his brother first, but a great leader thinks of all the people. Your warriors will respect you more for this."

"I am not a Chief, nor a leader."

"These warriors follow you before any other. Yes, my friend, whether you like it or not, you are a Chief to these warriors."

"And you Grey Badger?"

"My father had only one son. You have always been as a brother, since we were children chasing the rabbit. Since we were young warriors holding the horses for the older men. Yes, I, Grey Badger will follow you."

"You too, are as my brother. I worry about you as I do Wild Horse."

"I will ride ahead so we do not stumble into an enemy blindly."

Lone Eagle nodded as his friend rode away. Responsibility for these friends weighed heavily upon his mind. Perhaps he shouldn't have left Wild Horse behind. Thumping his horse harder than needed, he led his men towards the land of the Sioux. The shadows had grown long when Grey Badger returned to the raiding party. "I have seen nothing."

"That is good, we are making good time. The Crow will have to ride hard to catch us."

"And Wild Horse?"

"He has not returned." Lone Eagle looked behind them, worry sounding in his voice.

"He will come soon."

"We will rest the horses here then continue."

"It gets dark, maybe we should wait for Wild Horse here." Grey Badger had worry in his voice too.

"No, we will water the horses and continue."

"We should make good time in the dark."

"Yes, we should be in our village in three sleeps."

"Maybe, Grey Badger will wait for the young one."

"No, to treat him as a child would dishonor him!"

"Lone Eagle is right."

Wild Horse had tied his gelding in a secluded stand of trees back from where the Crow Warriors following should cross the river. Settling down to watch from his vantage point, he pulled out a piece of deer jerky. Looking back to where the horse was hidden, he judged the amount of time it would take him to reach the horse when the Crows appeared.

"Good, now I wait."

His jet black eyes were all business as he scanned the far bank. A few deer had come down to water earlier and he knew no riders were near yet. The sun rose higher and a swarm of flies had started settling on the concealed warrior. Wild Horse's attention had strayed to where a family of beaver' were busily building a dam across a small eddy, when the gelding snorted behind him. Sinking into the grass, Wild Horse waited, the hairs standing on the back of his neck. Surely the Crow dogs have not gotten behind me! He thought.

Suddenly two Crow riders appeared on the bank. Studying the ground at the crossing, they were not aware of the hidden warrior. Again the horse moved. Pushing himself carefully backwards Wild Horse crawled to where he could view the gelding. A Crow was slowly creeping towards the horse.

Notching an arrow, Wild Horse knew he would have to take this enemy first hoping no other was on this side of the river yet. The arrow flew true, its shaft sinking in the Crow's side almost to the feathers. Rising quickly Wild Horse was almost to the horse when another warrior threw himself at the running Sioux. Neither man had time to dodge the others knife and both blades found their marks. Wild Horse watched the Crow's face as it relaxed and the warrior crumpled slowly to the ground, the huge skinning knife protruding from his stomach. Sinking to one knee above the fallen warrior, Wild Horse took hold of the knife that was in his side and pulled it free.

"Aiyee my friend, your blade burns." Wild Horse muttered to the dead Crow. Feeling himself go faint from the pain he shook his head several times. "Do not go to sleep, the Crow women will have you over a warm fire."

Pulling the leather shirt from the dead Crow, Wild Horse threw it over his shoulder to be used later for a bandage for his side which was bleeding freely. Returning to his viewpoint he found the Crows were still sitting on the other bank. Probably waiting for their friends to signal them across, he thought. With two quick cuts he removed the dead warrior's top knots and eased onto the gelding.

"Lone Eagle will smile when I bring your scalps and ponies my friends."

Gathering up the two Crow ponies he turned away from the river and rode off quietly, but quickly as possible. Looking down at his bleeding side the warrior grinned. "Maybe Lone Eagle is right; you are foolish."

"Look, something stirs up dust in the valley." A warrior, posted as sentinel pointed to the valley below.

"Maybe it is Wild Horse." Grey Badger strained his eyes.

"My brother would not be so foolish as to stir the dust for the Crow to see."

"Perhaps buffalo." Another put in.

A few minutes passed and a rider leading two horses came down the valley at a dead run. "It is Wild Horse." Grey Badger nodded.

"Something is wrong, look at the way he rides, clinging to the horse." Whipping the gray stallion, Lone Eagle plunged down the rough trail leading to the valley floor. Grey Badger motioned for one of the warriors to hold the horses and followed. Catching the running horse' rawhide hackamore, Lone Eagle pulled the heaving gelding to a stop. A quick slash with his knife freed Wild Horse's hands where he had tied himself to the gelding's mane.

"Aiyee brother!" The youngster grinned weakly. "The Crow dogs follow; I think their women want me for their fires."

Quickly pulling the wounded warrior over on his horse, Lone Eagle started back the way he had come. Grey Badger led the tired horses. Arriving back with the waiting warriors, Lone Eagle eased Wild Horse into the waiting arms of a warrior.

"Is he hurt bad?" Grey Badger questioned.

"He has lost much blood. Tall Bear, take White Antelope and return down the valley and see where the Crows are, hurry."

"Yes, Lone Eagle."

"Do not go far and do not let them see you."

"Wild Horse is weak; if he travels he will die." A warrior spoke as he washed the wound.

Lone Eagle scanned the valley below, then lifted Wild Horse to the grays back. Mounting the horse behind Wild Horse, Lone Eagle supported the wounded man. Motioning Grey Badger forward, they started towards a heavily wooded area across the valley. Tall Bear and White Antelope joined them just as they forded a small, swift flowing stream crossing the valley.

"The Crows do not follow. They ride to the far end of the valley." Tall Bear motioned with his hands.

"Why would they go there?" Lone Eagle quizzed his scouts.

"I do not know. The tracks of Wild Horse were easy to see."

"Grey Badger, quickly go there and look." Lone Eagle pointed to the end of the valley.

The warrior thundered across the valley floor not worried about stirring up dust. The Crows knew they were somewhere to the east, it didn't matter if he was seen. Laying Wild Horse on the ground a warrior cleaned the bleeding wound again and dressed it from strips of the shirt.

"Wild Horse fought bravely to defeat two enemies with his knife." A warrior held up the two Crow scalps.

"Yes, my friend." Lone Eagle agreed, looking quietly at his brother.

"Grey Badger comes."

Lone Eagle waited for Grey Badger. The warrior's face was grim as he dismounted beside the waiting warriors. "They are there, just sitting on their horses, watching."

"Maybe more Crows come from the village?" A warrior questioned.

"No, the village is to the north."

"Another village perhaps?" White Antelope suggested.

"You have done well, Grey Badger." Lone Eagle praised his friend.

"What will we do?" White Antelope looked down the valley anxiously.

"There is a small trail that leads off to the east." Grey Badger nodded.

"We will take Wild Horse and go that way." Lone Eagle motioned.

Again Grey Badger took the lead as the raiders made their way warily along the small game trail. Climbing steadily from the valley, the riders stopped often to let Wild Horse rest and waited for Grey Badger to motion them forward. Near the top, Grey Badger suddenly appeared above them and turned his horse in circles. The riders quickly dispersed along the trail and waited for the scout to come to them.

"More Crows!"

"How would they get ahead of us?"

"I do not think they look for us. They have captives."

"Captives!" Lone Eagle was curious.

"White eye women."

"Then, that is why the other Crows wait."

"I think so, my friend."

On foot Lone Eagle and Grey Badger made their way back to the top of the trail. The war party of Yellow Moon, with Virginia and Elizabeth in tow, were passing just below where the two warriors were concealed.

"Yellow Moon!" Lone Eagle growled at the sight of his old enemy. "That is why the horse herd was unprotected; the Crow dog was raiding the whites.

"Why?" Grey Badger asked. "The Crows have always licked the white man's feet."

"Who can trust a Crow?"

"Aiyee, Lone Eagle, those are the white women from the fort."

"The one they call the Medicine Woman?"

"Yes, I seen her at the fort when I rode in with Wild Horse; she is the same, the red hair one cannot forget."

"More Crows!" Lone Eagle motioned down the valley.

"They are the ones that were following us."

Lone Eagle and Grey Badger watched as the oncoming Crows greeted the war party of Yellow Moon. From their vantage point they could see the heated gesturing of Yellow Moon as he berated the new arrivals. Lone Eagle thought the Crow Chief would strike out at the warriors, but suddenly he pulled his knife and made several cuts on his own arms.

"Ah, my friend, the Crow grieves." Lone Eagle smiled. "Maybe, one of the warriors Wild Horse killed might be a relative, even a son."

"That will make him even madder."

"Look; the Medicine Woman talks with Yellow Moon."

"She does not seem afraid."

"She must be as brave as the people say. Come we go." Lone Eagle said, leading the way back down to the waiting warriors.

"How is Wild Horse?" Grey Badger asked, kneeling beside the warrior.

"He sleeps, but he is very weak."

Sending Tall Bear to the rise to watch the Crows, Lone Eagle pulled Grey Badger off to the side. "We are in much danger, my friend."

"Yes, Wild Horse cannot travel and we cannot leave him."

"You must take the warriors and the horse's home, away from danger." Lone Eagle looked to where Wild Horse lay.

"And you?"

"I cannot leave my brother, and he cannot ride."

"Then I too, will stay."

"No my friend, you must do as I ask, there are too many Crows to fight; we are too few."

"What will Lone Eagle do?"

"I have a plan."

Hiding Wild Horse in a jumble of blown down trees and brush, the result of a bad spring storm, Lone Eagle led the rest of the warriors back to the top of the hill where they had last observed the Crows.

"What are they doing?"

"They talk while Yellow Moon mourns." Lone Eagle guessed. "They think they have us, and are in no hurry."

"They may be right." Grey Badger agreed.

Separating his warriors, Lone Eagle split the raiders into two groups. One would take the horses, the other group to pull the Crows off on a wild chase.

"The Crow ponies are tired. They will never be able to catch the buffalo runners. Tall Bear will take two men and go to the end of the valley and let the Crows see him. When the Crows give chase, you will lead the rest of the warrior's home."

"And you, Lone Eagle?" White Antelope asked.

"I will stay with Wild Horse until he can travel."

"What do we tell your father?"

"Tell him I will bring his sons home safe."

"My friend let me, Grey Badger, remain with Wild Horse, it is you who should lead the warrior's home."

"Thank you brother, but it is I who will stay."

"Hoka Hey, let us go tease the Crow dogs." Tall Bear motioned to the warriors, and with a nod to Lone Eagle, they rode towards the end of the valley.

"He is a brave man; let us remember this and sing his praises when we tell of our deeds." Lone Eagle watched the riders as they passed from sight.

"I will remember."

"Goodbye, my friend." Lone Eagle extended his hand.

"Goodbye. Take care of the young one."

Lone Eagle watched as Tall Bear rode into full view of the Crow warriors. He grinned as Tall Bear pretended terror and turned the buffalo runner with a scream.

"He plays the rabbit well." Grey Badger watched the Crows racing after Tall Bear and his men.

"They leave three warriors with the women."

"We go, goodbye again, my friend." Grey Badger led his men to the east leading the stolen horses behind them.

The three Crows guarding Virginia and Elizabeth spotted Grey Badger and his men leaving the ridge. Lone Eagle watched as one of the warriors raced off to tell Yellow Moon. Kneeing the gray stallion Lone Eagle skirted the timber that would bring him in behind the Crow. He had to cut the man off or Grey Badger would be in danger, as he didn't know the Crows had seen him leave. The thundering of the great stallion's hooves on the valley floor made the Crow look behind him. At the sight of Lone Eagle and the gray stallion of Yellow Moon, the warrior whipped his tired pony unmercifully. Sensing the Sioux was almost upon him, the Crow flung himself to the ground, reaching for an arrow and the bow that hung from his back.

"Ah, you are too slow, Crow dog." Lone Eagle yelled as the gray's shoulder knocked the warrior backwards.

Sliding from the stallion's back, Lone Eagle walked to where the fallen warrior was rising. Grabbing for the knife that hung at his side the Crow was trying to free it from its sheath when the knife of Lone Eagle cut the life from him.

"You should have stayed home with the women, Crow." Lone Eagle said disdainfully looking into the dying mans eyes.

Remounting the stallion he headed back up the valley towards the women. If it was indeed the medicine woman she could heal Wild Horse. The two warriors remaining with Virginia and Elizabeth had followed the valley the way Yellow Moon had gone, and were rounding a turn in the broad, flower speckled bottom when a warning from one of the Crows brought the party up short. Virginia and Elizabeth looked in the direction the warriors were looking. To their amazement a huge warrior, astride a beautiful gray horse, sat quietly in the meadow blocking their path. Sensing the alarm on the Crow's faces Virginia edged her horse closer to Elizabeth.

"Lone Eagle!" One of the warriors hissed.

At the mention of the name Virginia stared closer at the waiting warrior. This one was different, not dressed as the Crow. He had to be Sioux. "Phillip." The words whispered from her mouth.

"Lone Eagle, Phillip or whatever, he's the most magnificent thing I've ever seen." Elizabeth sighed.

The two crows had forgotten the women, and ridden out to face the lone warrior. Cocking the one rifle, they waited knowing the warrior would come. Elizabeth whipped her horse forward ramming the one with the rifle causing it to fire. Virginia watched, fascinated, as the warrior on the gray charged, his mighty war cry echoing up and down the valley.

The horse's speed was incredulous; she watched amazed as the warrior lay on the side of the horse when the rifle exploded, then popped back up unhurt. The gray was on the Crows, pushing the smaller horses back, knocking one to the ground. The huge warrior's knife hissed through the air imbedding itself into the down Crow's chest.

A choked off scream brought Virginia's attention from Lone Eagle's struggle to where Elizabeth stood over the other warrior, a bloody knife clutched tightly in her hand.

"Elizabeth! What..?"

"He needed help." Elizabeth cut her off sharply.

Lone Eagle walked to where Elizabeth stood over the fallen Crow. Taking the knife from her hand he looked into her face for a minute then motioned the two women to their horses. His gaze followed the back of the dark haired woman as she mounted her horse thinking to himself, these whites are indeed dangerous if their women all fight like this one.

Scalping the warriors, Lone Eagle led the horses to the north and across the small creek. Following it for a few minutes he would try and trick the Crows into thinking he was heading home. Mixing his tracks with the tracks of the other warriors he rode away then doubled back to where Wild Horse lay hidden.

"Still think he's Phillip?"

"He looks exactly the same as Bill."

"He is like him, in looks only. I don't think you'd see Bill cutting somebody's hair off."

Following Lone Eagle, they were amazed when he stopped at a wall of briars and brush and started pulling the maze apart. Making a path for them, they found they were in a small enclosure, almost impossible to see through. A warrior lay on the ground nearby. Kneeling beside Wild Horse, Lone Eagle motioned for Virginia to come close. Pointing at the man on the ground, Lone Eagle stepped back.

"Well, I'll say one thing for you, Virginia Lane, everyone out here seems to know you're a doctor." Elizabeth shook her head.

Virginia hadn't moved fast enough when Lone Eagle motioned for her, and received a shove from Lone Eagle that brought her to her knees. Elizabeth jumped between Lone Eagle and Virginia only to receive a slap from him that sent her reeling over a dead tree stump.

"Elizabeth, are you alright?"

"I'll say one thing for him, he hits harder than the others did." Virginia was amazed; this time Elizabeth didn't seem mad at all.

Another lighter shove from Lone Eagle brought Virginia to the side of Wild Horse. Pulling the rough bandages from the warriors wound she quickly examined him. Turning to where Lone Eagle stood she pushed sticks together indicating a fire. With a shake of his head Lone Eagle picked up the scalps of the Crows and shook them in her face.

"He's either going to scalp you or he's trying to tell you there's more Crows out there." Elizabeth, for once, wasn't joking.

"I know there's more out there." Virginia insisted on the fire again, this time drawing her finger across her throat and pointing at Wild Horse.

"He isn't going for a fire, Gin, do the best you can."

"I need water."

Elizabeth picked up the deer skin and motioned to the creek a short ways off. Snatching the skin from her, Lone Eagle made his way back through the jungle of briars and branches.

Running after him Virginia pointed to his knife and held her hand out. Hesitating, Lone Eagle looked to where Wild Horse lay then placed the knife in her hands. Returning with the water Lone Eagle and Elizabeth held the warrior down while Virginia finished stitching the wound closed. Elizabeth ripped up part of her dress for something to wrap the wound tight with. Exposing her leg she frowned when Lone Eagle ignored her.

"Elizabeth, I swear." Virginia said noticing the bared leg. "You're a tease."

"He didn't even look."

"Excuse me! I thought you were in love with Bill."

"Who said I wasn't?"

"Forget it." Virginia was exasperated.

Finishing with Wild Horse, Virginia felt his head then leaned back against a log and relaxed. Lone Eagle looked at his brother then walked to where Virginia sat. "Enjou!"

"I think he's trying to thank you." Elizabeth muttered.

Smiling she shook her head up at him. He was indeed quite a figure of a man, brother or not.

22

By late afternoon, Horatio had missed the girls but they had not returned to the fort. Seeing Virginia's medical bag missing, Horatio started Raven and Crow Foot looking for them while he walked to Lame Bull's village thinking Virginia might be held up doctoring one of the Sioux. Horatio knew Virginia to be headstrong, but she had never directly disobeyed him before. Maybe Lame Bull had sent for her and she didn't have time to tell him where she was going. No matter, he was used to being obeyed she would get a good piece of his mind when he found her.

Arriving at Lame Bull's lodge, Horatio found the old Chief and finally was able to make him understand he was looking for Virginia and Elizabeth. The two men walked through the village with Lame Bull, asking everyone if they had seen them. Finding no one who had, Lame Bull accompanied Horatio back to the fort. Seeing Raven and Crow Foot searching the grounds of the fort Colonel Dodd questioned both warriors as best he could. With some difficulty he finally was able to figure out the girls were missing. Immediately he dispatched a squad of dragoons to help in the search.

Everyone spread out around the fort and searched all the way to the river. Finding nothing, they returned to the fort as the night had turned pitch black. Lame Bull was finally able too make Horatio and the Colonel understand he would return with his warriors and best trackers when the sun came up. Horatio returned to the wagon and set around the campfire discussing the situation with Colonel Dodd. Raven and Crow Foot sat nearby, with a sad look on their faces. Horatio knew they might know something but the language barrier prevented him from being able to talk with them. Colonel Dodd had sent a soldier riding from the fort to bring back a local trapper who could speak the Sioux language.

If only Press and Bill, or Ed Monk was here. Never had the old general felt so helpless. Early the next morning, Lame Bull rode up to the fort with several of his warriors behind him. The trapper had arrived just ahead of Lame Bull and his men and was in council with them. Within minutes the Sioux trackers were spreading out and headed north and west.

"They figure it was Crow raiders Colonel, that's why they are looking to the north," the trapper explained as the warriors rode off.

"Crows, old one." Lame Bull announced to Horatio when the trackers returned.

"When?" Horatio questioned the interpreter.

"Yesterday; midday he says."

"Ask him where they will take them."

"South, to their country."

"Will they be harmed?" Horatio dreaded to hear the answer to his question.

"I can answer that one for you. I doubt it, or they wouldn't have left here with them. A Crow raiding party does not usually molest their captives, leastways not until they get them home." The trapper spoke up.

"Tell Lame Bull I'll pay many trade goods if his men can get them back."

"I don't think you should be doing that, General." The trapper shook his head.

"Why?"

"The Sioux hate the Crows and if they get in sight of them Crow warriors there's gonna be a big fight. Your women would probably be the first to die. That's why Lame Bull has kept his warriors from following."

Lame Bull listened to the two men then spoke up. "I will send a runner to Ishta Shakota; maybe he can get help from High Meadows and find women."

"Good, I will travel with him."

"You are old, my friend."

Horatio glared. "I'm not that old. If they have harmed those girls I'll personally raise an army and wipe them from this earth."

Lame Bull looked into the old warrior's eyes and knew now what Ishta Shakota said about this one was true. When riled he was indeed a great warrior. Immediately Horatio saddled the Cheyenne mare and grabbed his rifle and supplies. Raven and Crow Foot joined him as they followed the Sioux warrior from the fort. Colonel Dodd could only wish them luck and God speed.

No rest had been given the tired horses and to the amazement of the warriors it was the General who pushed the hardest. Two days later the staggering horses and tired men rode into the village of High Meadows. They had been spotted coming down into the valley and several armed warriors waited outside the village as they rode up.

Press, hearing the commotion stepped from Blue Thunder's lodge and was astounded to see Horatio being helped down from Virginia's lathered mare. Knowing something was bad wrong for the General to abuse a horse this way, he plunged through the crowd to Horatio's side. Too tired to speak, Horatio pointed to Raven and collapsed. Picking Horatio up bodily, Press carried him to where Bill lay. Calling for the squaw to tend Horatio, Press hurried back to where High Meadows, Tall Bow, and several warriors were questioning the Sioux warrior and Raven. Bill hobbled out of the lodge to listen to the gathered warriors.

"What's wrong?" Press asked urgently.

High Meadows explained what he had learned from the Sioux runner. Looking to Raven and Crow Foot they acknowledged what had happened and that the Medicine Woman was indeed stolen.

"I leave immediately." Press spoke to High Meadows. "My uncle, I need a guide to the Crow country."

"There are many Crows, my son."

"There are not enough Crows to stop me." The fire from Press' eyes made High Meadows nod his head.

"I understand; I too, once lost a woman to the Crow dogs."

"I will lead you, Ishta Shakota." Little Elk spoke up.

"We will go with you." Raven and Crow Foot stepped forward.

"I will have the fastest horses from my herds ready when you are." Tall Bow grimly told Press.

"Ishta Shakota thanks Tall Bow."

"I would send many warriors with you, but they are away hunting for the shaggy ones and Lone Eagle is now in Crow country." High Meadows told Press. "A few wish to go with you."

"Thank you a few will be enough to find the Crow Village." Press hurried to Blue Thunder's lodge to check on Horatio.

"I am going, too." Bill stood awkwardly, leaning on a crutch Press had fashioned him.

"Not this time old friend. You would just slow me down and I have to get to Virginia and Elizabeth as quick as possible."

"I understand."

Kneeling over the unconscious Horatio, Press placed his hand on the old one's shoulder. "He's just asleep from sheer exhaustion. I'll see after him." Bill spoke from outside the lodge.

"I'll be back soon with the girls. You take good care of yourself and the General."

"Good luck."

Grabbing his rifle and a few supplies, Press hurried to where Tall Bow waited with the horses and warriors. Besides the Cheyenne's and Little Elk, several other warriors waited already mounted. Swinging on to a horse bareback, Press looked down at High Meadows and nodded. "Thank you Uncle, Ishta Shakota will never forget what the Sioux people do for me this day, never." Squeezing the Chief's arm he waved at Tall Bow and Bill then left the village at a hard run, with Little Elk leading the way.

"Hoka Heye." Came from the warriors, as they thundered out of the village, the yells of the brave heart song carrying back to the people.

Press pushed the warriors like a man possessed until Little Elk warned him the horses could continue no further without rest. Realizing the truth in the young warrior's words Press called a halt by a clear stream of water. Unable to stand still, he paced back and forth until Little Elk gave the order to ride. Seeing the rage and worry in his eyes the warriors shook their heads. They weren't familiar with whites and this one had more hatred in him than any red man they had ever known. Press knew the warriors followed him on their own free will as no Sioux took orders from anyone unless they wanted to. He also knew that there were no braver fighters than the ones following him.

After three days of hard riding the horses were gaunt and not going much farther without food and rest. Luckily one of the Sioux warriors coming in from a scout reported smoke in the valley ahead. The warrior dismounted and told of finding a Snake hunting party camped a few miles distance.

"Maybe they know something of the girls." Press looked at Little Elk.

"They are allies of the Crow, but I don't think so, they are just hunting the shaggies."

"Maybe they know something." Press insisted.

"What does Ishta Shakota wish?" Little Elk asked, watching Press close.

"How many are there?"

"Six, Mighty Heart." The warrior spoke respectfully.

"We will talk with them." Press mounted his horse and started for the Snake camp.

The scout had been right, six warriors lay about their camp sprawled on blankets and talking. They had not put out a lookout thinking they were in Crow country and safe. Before he could be stopped, Press rode forward alone into the camp. Many stories are still told about the tenacity of the Mighty Heart after the Snakes laughed at his question as to the whereabouts of Virginia and Elizabeth.

None of the warriors behind Press had time to get into the fight as Ishta Shakota, in his rage, killed or ran off all six of the Snake warriors. Watching in awe at the ferocity of the Mighty Heart One, they knew his medicine was strong and he was indeed a brave warrior. They would now follow him against the entire Crow Nation if he asked. Three of the Snake warriors were dead so fast the others shrank before the demon that had set upon them. Turning, they had fled with the Sioux warriors in pursuit. Only one of the Snakes was captured alive and he had a broken arm. The Sioux had dispatched the others in a frenzy of blood lust after watching Press kill the others.

Bringing their prisoner before Press, they pushed him forward. "Ask him again about the women." Press spoke to Little Elk. The Snake spit on the ground in front of Press, as he came to understand what the white eye wanted to know.

"Tell him I will cut him into little pieces if he doesn't tell me what I want to know."

Again the Snake muttered something and spit. Press stepped closer, pulling his knife, and swiftly as a striking rattlesnake sliced the man's right ear off. "Ask him again."

Again Little Elk asked and again the Snake said nothing. Press's knife slashed again and the warrior's loin cloth fell to the ground, a thin line of blood showing where the knife had struck too close.

"Tell him, this is his last chance. If he doesn't answer he won't need a squaw again, but I will let him live as a gelding." Press wasn't bluffing and the warrior knew it as his eyes widened.

Press grabbed the man's privates and poised the knife. Cowering, the man started talking before the knife could do its bloody work. Press read the sign language as the man spoke.

"He says a demon rescued the women."

"What does he mean, Little Elk?" Press asked the young warrior.

"This I do not know."

"Where is this valley he speaks of?"

"He says it is a day's hard ride to the north."

"We will go there."

"What of this coward?" Little Elk questioned.

Blood spurted everywhere as Press slit the man's stomach open then cut his heart out. Silently, the Sioux warriors watched as Press kicked the body away from him and mounted his gelding. Any Sioux who thought the whites a weak race changed their minds after watching the way Ishta Shakota's eyes spit fire as he killed the last Snake warrior.

There was no mercy in this one, and any enemy who came afoul of him was going to pay until his blood cooled. Press pushed on north riding through the night as if the devil himself was after him. The warriors were dead tired, but still the Mighty Heart one pushed on and they followed. None uttered a word, just followed as if Press was Lone Eagle himself. Nearing daylight, at Little Elks insistence, Press called a halt where there was plenty of grass and water for the tired horses. The Sioux quickly hobbled their horses on the good grass near the creek. Collapsing on the soft ground they fell instantly asleep, leaving only Press and Little Elk watching over them.

"You should sleep, Little Elk; I will watch."

"I will, but first I would speak with you."

"I know of what you wish to speak." Press turned his head.

"A good leader does not push his warriors so hard."

"I know Little Elk, and no leader could ask for better men than these." Press nodded. "We will rest."

"Enjou, now Little Elk can sleep."

"Little Elk."

"Yes."

"Thank you, I will never forget, however this turns out."

Press stood guard the rest of the night thinking only of Virginia in the hands of a demon, or whatever the Snake warrior meant. Seeing Press still on guard when they awoke several of the warriors protested that he had not awakened them. Quieting them with an upraised hand, he walked among them letting his eyes rest on each warrior. Nodding at Crow Foot and Raven he spoke to the warriors.

"No matter what we find today, my brothers, I thank you. No man is better on the war trail than you. I am a stranger to most of you and yet you follow me into danger without protest. I thank you, and I am forever in your debt." The Sioux warriors were not used to such sentimental words, but knowing the bravery of Ishta Shakota they understood he was paying them the deepest respect. And their respect for him grew even more.

"We will ride the Snake horses and let ours rest today." Little Elk spoke then led the war party on towards the valley, while watching closely for enemy warriors.

Almost three days had passed since Virginia had treated Wild Horse's wounds, and still the fever raged inside the young warrior's body. Lone Eagle had foraged after dark bringing in food for the women and horses. Virginia watched closely as Elizabeth and Lone Eagle seemed to spend more time together, trying to converse, sometimes breaking into quiet laughter. The Crows had not come near their hiding place. Just once, a small war party had passed pricking up the ears of the horses. Lone Eagle and the women had quickly clapped their hands over the horse's muzzles to keep them from whinnying, and giving their hiding place away.

"Isn't he something?" Elizabeth said dreamily to Virginia, as Lone Eagle passed by watering the horses.

"And Bill?" Virginia spoke sharply to Elizabeth.

"He's handsome too, but in a different way."

"Are you in love with Phillip?"

"Why, Virginia Lane, I never, I'm engaged to Bill or have you forgotten?" Elizabeth looked shocked.

"I haven't forgotten, I just wondered if you have."

"I certainly have not."

"Good, because I don't intend to lose a brother, or maybe both, over a woman who can't make up her mind!" Virginia was serious.

A groan brought both women's attention to where the wounded warrior lay; his feverish eyes studying them closely. Moving to his side, Virginia reached to feel for fever when suddenly the warrior's hand crushed strongly around her wrist. Virginia stared calmly into the deep dark eyes unflinching.

"She is the Medicine Woman, my brother, and she has saved your life." The words from Lone Eagle, who had slipped in quietly, caused Wild Horse to release his hold on Virginia.

Lifting the wounded warriors head, Virginia dribbled some cool water down his parched throat from her cupped hand. Nodding, the warrior muttered something which Virginia took to be a thank you, then closed his eyes. Lone Eagle moved to his brother's side and felt of his forehead. Turning to Virginia, he laid his hand on her shoulder momentarily, pulling it away just as quickly.

"I thought she was a Crow squaw with her knife." Wild Horse opened his eyes and grinned weakly.

"She is from the fort." Lone Eagle answered.

"Too thin, you need a fatter woman."

"Wild Horse!" Lone Eagle could just shake his head. Close to dying, this one would have to say something about a woman.

"He thinks a lot of this young man." Elizabeth said watching the softness come over Lone Eagle's face.

"Yes he does; I think this must be the younger son of Tall Bow, the one Monk spoke of." Virginia agreed.

23

After finding the warriors that Lone Eagle had killed, and the women missing, Yellow Moon had followed the trail of Lone Eagle and the women until he thought they were headed east towards Sioux hunting grounds. Knowing his tired horses would never overtake the faster buffalo runners, and overcome by grief, the Crow Chief had decided to return to his village to bury his son whom Wild Horse had killed in the horse raid; also to bury his white father Gordon, whom the stomach sickness had killed.

No one had told him of the loss of his prize gray stallion. This news had been the breaking point, causing Yellow Moon to lose whatever control he had of his temper, causing a temporary wild insanity to take over his thinking. Now all he could think of was revenge against Lone Eagle and the Sioux People, who he held responsible for all of his misfortunes. Sending runners to his allies, the Snakes, Yellow Moon started preparing his warriors to ride to the village of High Meadows. Both tribes would meet at the big river and then descend on the Sioux village. High Meadows and his village would perish under the hooves of the Crow and Snake war ponies.

Lone Eagle heard the steady rhythm of horses coming up the valley and rushed to the entrance of the deadfall and peered out. Several minutes passed before the first movement came from the west end of the valley.

"Crows!" Lone Eagle hissed to the women then rushed to keep the horses quiet. The least little noise would carry on the wind and bring the Crow screaming like banchees down on their hiding place.

"Yellow Moon!" Virginia whispered to Lone Eagle who peered out at the colorful warriors spread out across the valley, coming towards them at an easy lope. The Crow Chief was out front leading at least a hundred Crow and Snake warriors.

The war party passed by the windfall without a glance at their hideaway, causing the women to let out a sigh of relief. Lone Eagle knew by the war paint and the amount of warriors, both Crow and Snakes, Yellow Moon was riding on the village of High Meadows. He knew if he did not warn the village his people would be slaughtered. This was no pony raid, with the Snakes along and Yellow Moon in black paint; it meant the Crow Chief was in mourning.

Perhaps one of the warriors Wild Horse had killed was the son of Yellow Moon. The Crow was headed for the Ogallala Village to have his revenge on his long time enemies the Sioux. The village had to be warned, but Wild Horse could not ride, and the women would have to be left unprotected also.

Lone Eagle walked to where Wild Horse lay. The warrior's breathing was easier and his face had regained some of its color. "What is it, my brother?" Wild Horse had heard the pounding of the horses as they passed, and saw the worried look on Lone Eagle's face.

"You are awake?"

"I felt the earth tremble like buffalo running."

"Crows!"

"Crows here?" Wild Horse tried to rise.

"No brother, they have passed." Lone Eagle eased the warrior back to the ground.

"That is good; I am too tired to fight with them today."

"Rest, Wild Horse, soon we will be back in our village."

"Yes, and then I will buy a pretty woman as I promised, but perhaps you have already found one. I have seen you look at the raven haired squaw." Wild Horse grinned.

"She is a white woman."

"That's true, but I have watched your eyes follow her when she walks."

"She is beautiful, and brave as well."

"Then you will keep her for your lodge?" Wild Horse asked.

"Sleep my brother. We will talk when you wake."

Feeling a hand on his shoulder, Lone Eagle stood and turned to face Virginia. Hearing her speak and motion to the east, Lone Eagle knew she was telling him to go to his people. How did she know what was on his mind? Maybe her medicine told her. Looking to the entrance of the deadfall, he saw Elizabeth holding the rein of the gray stallion.

"Yes, these white women were brave." Lone Eagle thought, knowing if he left they would be alone with a wounded man and no weapons. To leave would mean almost certain death for his brother, the Medicine Woman, and a woman he had looked upon as he had no other. To stay would mean death for his people. He understood his feelings for the raven haired woman even though she was white, but his feelings for the Medicine Woman was almost the same as he had for Wild Horse; this he couldn't understand.

He knew what his decision would be, but he knew when he rode out his life would never be the same. Still he could not let his people be massacred even if it meant their lives. Kneeling beside Wild Horse, he was about to explain why he was going when the gray stallion nickered. Lunging to his feet he clamped a strong hand over the stallion's muzzle.

"Ah, my beauty, you have betrayed me before we could hunt the buffalo together." Lone Eagle whispered to the stud as several riders rode towards them.

Preparing his bow and arrows, Lone Eagle was shocked when Virginia ran from the deadfall and waved at the approaching horsemen. Looking closer he was amazed when he recognized several warriors from his village with a white man. Watching, he saw the Medicine Woman throw herself into the arms of the white.

"Press, oh Press."

"Gin." Press gathered the little red head in his arms. "Are you alright?"

"Yes, Phillip, Lone Eagle saved us."

"Lone Eagle?" Press looked to where a large warrior and Elizabeth were exiting the brush pile, leading a magnificent gray stallion. The Sioux warriors gathered around Lone Eagle firing questions at him. Little Elk walked amongst them and harangued them for standing out in the open, like a herd of buffalo, for their enemies to see. Seeing the wisdom of his words, the warriors with Press and Virginia, quickly retreated to the safety of the windfall. Several warriors gathered around Wild Horse and started talking to him.

Virginia quickly told Press about Yellow Moon and his warriors, and that she thought they were headed for the village of Lone Eagle. Press stepped in front of Lone Eagle.

"For what you have done for the Medicine Woman, I thank you; now if she is right you must hurry to warn the village." Press extended his hand. Lone Eagle hesitated, then slowly reached forward awkwardly and grasped the strong hand of Ishta Shakota.

"I have heard of the good heart of Ishta Shakota towards the people, and my warriors tell me of your bravery against the Snakes. It is I who thank you Mighty Heart, for without the Medicine Woman, Little Elk would have died. We will talk more and smoke the pipe, but now I must hurry to warn my people."

Press quickly interpreted Lone Eagle's words for Virginia and Elizabeth. "Tell him I go with him." Elizabeth spoke up.

"You will stay with Wild Horse and the Medicine Woman." Lone Eagle answered her quietly when Press had translated.

"I go with you." Elizabeth walked to her horse.

"Are all white women so headstrong?" Lone Eagle asked Press.

"Some are."

"And I go with you, Preston Forbes."

"Yes ma'am, you do." Press grinned at Virginia.

Seeing the set faces of the women, Lone Eagle nodded and turned to where Wild Horse lay propped against a tree stump. "My brother, we must hurry to save the village from the Crow who would destroy our people. I will leave warriors to protect you and bring you home slowly, but now I must go fast." Lone Eagle spoke gently, grave concern in his voice.

Press was amazed. Was this the ferocious Lone Eagle he had heard so much about?

"Leave only one warrior with me. You will need the rest to fight the Crow dogs." Wild Horse answered weakly.

"I will not leave you defenseless."

"If we are discovered, it will not matter. Leave one and go fast brother; I will see you soon."

"When the village is safe, I will return for you." Turning, Lone Eagle faced his warriors. "My friends we must go quickly to our village. The horses must not be spared. I know you have traveled far and are weary, but we must hurry for if we do not do so your families will be destroyed by the Crow dogs I have set against you."

Press listened to the words of Lone Eagle, and watched as the tiredness seemed to lift from the listening warriors. He knew now, hearing the words of Lone Eagle, why the Sioux held him in such esteem. Here was a born leader.

Lone Eagle led the small band of warriors to the east in a hard lope. The extra horses that had been taken from the Snake warriors would enable them to change horses and travel faster.

He intended to beat Yellow Moon to the village, if it was possible, and warn High Meadows. The Crows had a big lead but he would try if there was any way; his people had to be warned.

Lone Eagle figured Grey Badger and the warriors he had sent ahead should be at the village to help, in case he didn't get there ahead of the Crows.

"You push the horses hard, my Chief." Little Elk rode up beside Lone Eagle.

"We must reach the village before Yellow Moon and his warriors." Lone Eagle growled at the young warrior.

"Without the ponies we will not be able to help anybody." The young warrior argued causing Lone Eagle to look over at him.

Pulling the gray stallion down to a walk Lone Eagle glared at Little Elk then slowly nodded his head. "You are right. How are you called?"

"I am Little Elk, from Lame Bull's village."

"You are wise, for one so young."

"If Lone Eagle did not worry for his people, he would not push them so."

Darkness came, and still Lone Eagle led the Sioux towards the east. Warriors switched horses, trying to save them all they could. Lone Eagle knew Yellow Moon; he had fought him before. The Crow, in his mourning, would ride his horses to death knowing he would get more at the Sioux village after he had plundered it. But Little Elk was right. If he killed their horses they would arrive too late to help the village.

As the sun showed itself in the east Lone Eagle called a halt near water. The women slid to the ground exhausted.

"Should we put out watchers my Chief?" A warrior asked Lone Eagle.

"Rest, the Crows look ahead at our village; they will not be looking behind them."

"You have traveled well, Ishta Shakota." Lone Eagle walked to where Press was giving the women jerky to eat.

"And you have led well, we make good time."

"And the women?"

"They are tired."

"Yes, but they are strong, worthy to be Sioux."

"They are that."

"The Medicine Woman, is she your squaw?"

"Soon, perhaps."

"She has strong medicine, she has saved Wild Horse, my brother."

"Her brother too."

"Can a Sioux warrior be her brother?"

"The Look Alike One and Lone Eagle has the same blood in them as the Medicine Woman, so if Wild Horse is your brother, he is the brother of the Medicine Woman too." Press answered watching the face of Lone Eagle. To his surprise Lone Eagle said nothing, only nodded.

"You know?" Press asked.

"Yes, I have heard of the Look Alike One, the one that looks the same as I, and when I looked upon the Medicine Woman I felt something I could not understand."

"Then you know your blood is not Sioux, but white." Press knew he was on touchy ground, but he had to ask now and try to make Lone Eagle understand why they were here.

"My blood may have been white at birth, but my heart is Sioux. My soul is Sioux and my people are Sioux."

"This is so my brother, but can you deny your blood people and your white skin?"

"Yes, where the sun does not reach I am lighter than most, but I am still Lone Eagle, son of the Sioux, brother of the Cheyenne, and enemy of the Crows and ..." Lone Eagle did not finish.

"The whites?" Press questioned.

"I have great respect for Ishta Shakota, but do not make us enemies, my friend." Lone Eagle warned.

"I, too, have great respect for Lone Eagle. No, we will never be enemies, for when I marry the Medicine Woman we will be brothers, and I could never find two men who I would rather call brother than you and the Look Alike One." Press held out his hand again to Lone Eagle.

Taking Press' hand, Lone Eagle shook it for the second time, only this time encircling it the Indian way. "This will stay between us."

"Yes, between us."

"The raven haired woman, does she have a man?"

"She is promised to the Look Alike One."

"Has her father accepted his ponies?"

"No."

"And he will not."

"How does Lone Eagle know this?"

"She has looked at me."

Press nodded his head but did not try to explain Elizabeth's flirtatious and teasing ways, for he knew Lone Eagle would not understand, or, like any man, want to. He could see as stoic as Lone Eagle was he was smitten with her.

"This may be so, my friend, but promise me one thing."

"What does Ishta Shakota wish?"

"That no matter who the raven haired one chooses there will be no bad feelings between you and the Look Alike One."

"He means much to you?"

"Both of you are as my brothers."

"Then I give you my word; it will be as you ask."

"Thank you."

"The Look Alike One has the advantage though." Lone Eagle grinned.

"How's that?"

"The woman, she does not speak Sioux."

"I have always heard love has no barriers."

"Perhaps you are right."

"I could always translate for you." Press laughed liking Lone Eagle more with every word. This brought a smile of amusement to the warrior's face. The strange conversation ended as Lone Eagle walked away to where Little Elk sat.

"What was that all about?" Virginia asked from where she rested.

"You don't want to know." Press shook his head.

"I already know, Elizabeth." Press looked at her amazed.

Press watched as Lone Eagle had a few words with the young warrior, who then selected one of the fresher horses and disappeared into the trees across the stream. After a short two hour rest the party was once again mounted and headed east at a ground eating trot.

Lone Eagle pushed the horses and riders hard all day, stopping only for water at the many small streams they crossed. The hard riding was beginning to show as Elizabeth and Virginia both had to be prodded to stay up. The horses were too tired to carry double, so the women had to ride by themselves. Staying awake and upright on the back of their horses was all they could manage. Though not wanting to slow the warriors, Press knew he would have to stop soon and let the women rest. Urging his tired horse faster, Press rode alongside the gray stallion.

"The gray never seems to tire." Press commented, looking at the stallion.

"He is indeed, a great one."

"It is not the same with the women."

"I know. We will stop at the river ahead and let the women rest." Lone Eagle looked back to where the women were riding.

"We do not wish to slow you from getting back to the village. You should go on and let us follow."

"No, we are close to the Sioux hunting grounds now. It is not much farther to the village, we will all go together. The horses and men need rest, too, if they are going into battle."

"Lone Eagle does not seem to be tired."

"Yes, I am tired, but I cannot show weakness or my warriors will lose faith in me."

Watching and listening to Lone Eagle, Press realized he had completely drawn the wrong picture in his mind of the warrior. Despite his outward appearance and the tales told about him, Lone Eagle had a gentleness and caring side that Bill lacked. His people came before himself in all things. This one would sacrifice himself for the good of the Sioux. Maybe this is what Bill was lacking. Somehow the General had made Bill hard, and had given him everything he needed in life except a caring heart. Bill loved his immediate family, and would die for them, but Lone Eagle's concern for the people went farther, deeper and with greater compassion.

Dismounting in a stand of willows, Lone Eagle had the men water, and then hobble the horses on the lush green grass along the rivers edge, but close in if needed. The tired party had barely sunk to the soft ground when Little Elk rode into camp and dismounted.

"Ah, Lone Eagle has made good time." Little Elk knelt beside the small fire they had burning.

Seeing the fatigue in the young warrior's face and knowing he had not eaten, Lone Eagle produced some jerky and handed it to him. "Eat Little Elk, then, we will talk."

"My stomach thanks you. It has grown smaller, and grumbles like a mad squaw in a small lodge." Little Elk smiled, wolfing down the jerky.

"Have you seen the village, or the Crow dogs?"

"Yes, they are camped where the deep canyon forms at the river. The village has not been disturbed and I did not go in and warn them. I thought if they started acting like they were alerted, the Crows would attack before you could arrive."

"You did well; have the Crows been scouting the village?"

"I do not know this, but they have been scouting you."

"Then they know we follow?" Lone Eagle was alarmed.

"Yes, and how many there are of us." Press added.

"I think Yellow Moon will send warriors back to attack you at the river." Little Elk continued.

"You are sure of this?"

"Yes, my Chief. I hid as several Crow scouts passed by. Their tracks showed where they have been watching you from there." Little Elk pointed to a stand of cedars a mile distant.

"Why would he do that?" A warrior asked.

"He knows I am here and he wishes to keep us from the village." Lone Eagle answered.

"Where will he attack?" Another spoke up.

"That I do not know. It does not matter; we must ride to help the village." A hardness came over Lone Eagle's face as he stood and gathered the gray's rein. "Thank you Little Elk; you have done well."

"I will ride ahead." Little Elk swung on a fresh horse and turned east towards the village.

Lone Eagle watched the young warrior disappear then led his warriors in pursuit. Press knew Lone Eagle's only thought now was getting to the village as quickly as possible. All day they traveled, coming to the little river with the deep canyons at sundown. No sign of Little Elk had been found. Only sheer will and determination kept the warriors and women going. Now fatigue had finally stopped them. Lone Eagle on the gray stallion seemed to be the only one able to continue. He knew his warriors and the women would have to rest. Tomorrow they would cross the swift waters of the river and reach the village.

Dismounting, Lone Eagle stooped over a still warm campfire and nodded. "Yellow Moon has let us catch up."

"How near is he?" Press asked.

"Not far, he can still reach the village before us, but we will be there to help." Lone Eagle looked to the east. "His warriors are as tired as we are."

"Little Elk should be here by now." Press was worried.

Lone Eagle looked solemnly at the ground. "Little Elk will not return to us."

Press studied the warrior's face and knew his prediction was true. Little Elk would have returned by now if he could. He didn't know how Lone Eagle knew, but he could feel it himself.

"How far to the village?" Press asked.

"If our horses were strong we could be there before the great one is overhead but." The warrior shrugged his shoulders. "We will cross the river when the great one returns."

Morning found the warriors mounted, and eager to follow Lone Eagle into the deep water. The river was up a little and the horses would be in deep water on this side, but the river was narrow and the horses would only have to swim a few feet before they could touch bottom.

"We have come far my friends, the village is near and our enemies are near."

"Lead us, Lone Eagle, we will follow." A warrior spoke up.

"First, we must cross the river. I believe the Crow will be waiting." Lone Eagle looked to where Press sat his horse beside Elizabeth and Virginia. "What does Ishta Shakota think?"

Press kneed his horse forward. "It is a good place for the Crow to attack as you come out of the river."

"What would you have us do?"

"Is there no other crossing?" Press asked, looking at the high banks up and down the river.

"There is, but we do not have time to ride there. We must cross here and ride to the village."

"Then go, but first, let me get to the ridge where I can cover you with my rifle."

Lone Eagle watched as Press dismounted and gave Virginia the reins to his sorrel then scrambled up a small knoll and laid down. Laying his rifle, powder horn, and shot beside him Press was ready and nodded down to the waiting warriors. Press studied the river's edge; nothing moved. He had a good view, and a good field of fire. His rifle could not miss at this range.

Lone Eagle looked at his warriors and nodded. "Hoka Heye, my brothers. It is a good day to die."

The horses eased off into the swift water and started swimming for the far bank. The gray touched bottom and waded from the deep, fast moving water into the shallows. Everything was quiet on the far bank, and nothing was moving near the trees. Press thought Lone Eagle had been wrong about the attack. Suddenly, down the sandy bank, a lone Crow warrior rode almost to the Sioux warriors then flung the mutilated body of Little Elk from his horse.

Shocked, Press looked at the young warrior's body. "This one's for you Little Elk." He spit as he rested the sights of the Hawkins fifty on the chest of the Crow waving Little Elk's scalp.

The Crow was torn from his horse as the large caliber ball tore through his chest. Crows swarmed from the timber and charged Lone Eagle and his warriors. Another Crow went down from the Hawkins, then another as Press reloaded and fired again. Arrows from the Sioux riding out of the river started knocking the Crows from their horses. This was not a game of counting coup; the Sioux were deadly with their aim. Again the rifle boomed from the far bank, another Crow went down, demoralizing the Crow warriors. Turning back towards the trees they fled from the terrible menace behind them.

The Sioux, their war clubs brandishing, followed, but their horses were done in, unable to catch the fleeing Crows. Lone Eagle held up his hand and called back his warriors. Telling them to catch the loose Crow horses, he waited on Press and the women. Watching Elizabeth plunge into the swift current of the river and swim her horse across, he nodded.

"A lot of woman, one who will keep a man's blood hot." He thought to himself as he watched her.

"Ishta Shakota has given us a great victory today." Lone Eagle praised Press. "Now we will hurry to the village."

"The white man's weapons are not all bad." Press grinned, holding up the Hawkins.

"That would depend on who's holding it." Lone Eagle looked to where the bodies of the dead Crows lay.

"That is true my friend, but remember in the days ahead the bow will be no match for the white man's rifle."

Lone Eagle nodded. "You have avenged Little Elk today; we will come for his body when the Crows are defeated."

"He was too young to die." Virginia spoke to Press.

"He earned much glory today, he will never die." Press translated Lone Eagle's words.

The last of the horse's strength was used up as Lone Eagle made his final dash for the village. Separating his small force, he sent warriors with Press to the west of the village hidden by a small draw, and the rest went with Lone Eagle to the high ridge above the village. Virginia and Elizabeth stayed with Lone Eagle. The high ridge would keep them safely out of danger should the battle turn back down the valley.

"Why does Yellow Moon wait to attack? The great one is now beginning to run the shadow world away." A warrior asked Lone Eagle.

"This I do not know, but it has saved the village; now we will be able to help."

"From here we will get to see the fighting, isn't it thrilling?" Elizabeth sat straighter on her horse.

"Thrilling? Elizabeth Hudson!" Virginia was astounded at the words. "That's the awfullest thing I've ever heard you say."

"Why?'

"People will die here today and you're thrilled."

"Yes, people will die today, they already have or have you forgotten, but doesn't it make you feel alive?"

"Heaven help her." Virginia frowned.

Elizabeth smiled, a flush coming over her cold face. The weather had turned colder and the expected snows had started. Flakes had started drifting across the valley during the night, slowly covering the ground.

"I'll be here to watch my man fight." Elizabeth looked at Lone Eagle.

"Which man?"

"The best man!" Elizabeth looked straight into Virginia's eyes.

"Sometimes Elizabeth, you exasperate me to no end." Virginia scolded.

"Don't you feel it Gin? The excitement, adventure." Elizabeth was truly excited.

"No, Elizabeth, I don't. Some of us, maybe all of us will die today and you're excited." Virginia was truly astounded at Elizabeth's attitude.

24

The early snows had started falling on the village, so Bill had retreated back into the warm comfort of the old squaw's lodge to work on the hackamore he was making out of horsehair. Several young boys sat at his feet and marveled at the way the Look Alike One could weave the hair so expertly into different shapes. Some just stared at the huge giant of a man and wondered at how much he looked like Lone Eagle. From time to time Bill would stop and scratch at his broken leg, being careful not to let the old woman see him. The leg had started to heal, and itch, driving him crazy at times. The squaw would severely reprimand him if she caught him scratching at it.

In spite of himself Bill was slowly picking up the Lakota language spoken to him continually by the young boys who surrounded him constantly. Smiling to himself he wondered what Elizabeth would think, seeing him now.

"Must be getting soft in the head." Bill muttered to himself.

"Speak Lakota." One of the older boys complained when he couldn't understand.

"You speak American." Bill laughed. He had been trying to get the young ones to speak English, and to shorten his name to Bill.

Whatever their interpretation for the Look Alike One was, it was long and he couldn't pronounce it. But try as he might he couldn't get them to say Bill. Nodding his head he picked up the hackamore and started braiding. Horatio had recovered fully from the long ride to the village, and when he wasn't with Bill, he stayed in the company of High Meadows and Tall Bow. Bill wondered how they communicated with each other, but seeing them walking through the village pointing and gesturing, he knew somehow they could. Horatio still worried about Virginia and Elizabeth, but he knew Press would somehow bring them home safely.

Several days had passed since Press and the warriors had left the village. Not a word had been heard since they departed. Some of the warriors who had been with Lone Eagle had returned, bringing many of the beautiful buffalo runners, stolen from the Crows, with them.

Grey Badger had related their story of the stealing of the horses, and how Wild Horse had gotten wounded, and the scalps and glory he had earned, and that he had seen the women captives in the hands of the hated Yellow Moon. He knew little else as Lone Eagle sent him on to the village, only that Lone Eagle said he would bring both of Tall Bow's sons home safe.

Grey Badger had asked High Meadows to go back and help with Wild Horse, but the old Chief had refused. Too many warriors were away from the village looking for the buffalo, and several warriors had left with Press to look for the women. No, the remaining able bodied warriors must stay and defend the women and helpless ones.

High Meadows had waited until the last possible moment to send out the hunters. Sensing the early winter snows upon them, he reluctantly sent them out to look for the herds that would sustain the tribe through the hungry and cold times ahead. High Meadows had sat in council with the elders and Blue Thunder, then ordered the horse herds brought in close to the village so the people could be ready to move quickly when the buffalo were found. Grey Badger had entered the old squaw's lodge once to stare at Bill, and remark something, which Bill thought was about the hackamore he was making. Perhaps curiosity had brought the warrior, Bill did not know. Picking up the hackamore, Bill shrugged and started braiding.

The pounding of a horse's hooves on the hard packed ground as it hurried through the village caused Bill to pull the flap of the lodge back and peer outside. One of the horse herders pulled his horse to a hard stop in front of High Meadow's lodge. Bill hobbled outside as the youth disappeared inside.

Quickly, many people were gathering. Seeing Horatio coming towards him faster than usual, Bill reached back inside for his crude made crutch.

"What has happened, Grandfather?"

"I do not know, but I understood enough that the Chief wants every man at his lodge." Bill started walking towards High Meadow's lodge when he felt a pair of strong hands take his arm and help him. Nodding his thanks to the warrior, Grey Badger, the three men hurried to the lodge.

Stepping inside Bill noticed how few fighting age men were actually left in the village. Forgetting all protocol, High Meadows stood and faced his warriors.

"My friends, the village is in grave danger. Our enemies the Crow, and their Snake dogs, are camped just outside the pass that leads into our valley. The father sun is up, soon they will attack." High Meadows raised his arms as everyone started speaking at once. "Quiet, we must think and act quickly. Luckily one of our herders was looking for a horse and came upon them without being seen."

"Then, my Chief, they do not know we have seen them as yet?" Grey Badger asked."

"No, they wait for something."

"I will go see these warriors."

"Go quickly Grey Badger, we will prepare."

Bill had learned enough Sioux from the young boys to understand a little of what was happening. Turning to Horatio he explained what little he understood.

"Then the village is going to be attacked." Horatio looked at the scared faces of the women and old ones, the warriors scrambling for their weapons, and knew. He had seen and been involved in war his whole life, these people were preparing for battle.

Walking back to their lodge, Horatio helped Bill inside then went about gathering up his weapons. Placing a rifle beside Bill, the old warrior stepped lightly back outside as the sun came up over the tree tops.

A few minutes passed and Grey Badger rode back into the village. "They are there waiting, many times our numbers." The warrior pointed his finger to the north end of the pass.

"What do they wait for?" High Meadows stared to where the warrior pointed.

"Soon they will come. Warriors came in just now from the north, and joined them. They looked as if they have been in a fight, several are bleeding."

"Lone Eagle?" Tall Bow questioned.

"If it was Lone Eagle, he would be here to fight."

"Even Lone Eagle could not defeat all that came riding in." Grey Badger did not say more.

"Grey Badger speaks the truth." Another warrior spoke up. "Perhaps he is dead."

"Do we fight? Or do we flee with the women and children." High Meadows asked.

"Fight, fight, fight." Came the roar from the warriors.

"What of the women and children?" Blue Thunder spoke up.

"The younger women and older boys will fight; the rest will hide in the woods until we come for them."

Bill had listened to all that was being said, but could only understand a little. Leaning calmly against his back rest he watched as Horatio strapped on his cutlass. The old warrior seemed to mumble beneath his breath. "One more time old friend, one more time."

Bill wished Press and Ed Monk was here. It was going to be a lively fight if he understood correctly what was being said. Their help would come in mighty handy. Smiling, he called to the old squaw.

"Scared lad?" Horatio had leaned back through the flap of the lodge and was studying Bill's face.

"No, I only wish I knew if Press had found Virginia and Elizabeth."

"Me, too." Horatio stepped back outside. Inside he heard Bill say something to the old squaw, then start whistling softly to himself.

"Scared? That boy doesn't know the meaning of the word." Horatio grinned. "Too bad he hadn't been in the big war with Andy Jackson to show his mettle."

The snow was coming harder, big flakes drifting quietly down, blanketing the valley. The children of the Ogallala were bundled up, along with the women and old people, and hurried off to the safety of the deep timber, away from the oncoming battle. The rest of the younger women joined the men at the end of the village where the Crow and Snake warriors were expected to appear. After Horatio left to join the gathered villagers, Bill summoned the old squaw to bring him the clothes he needed. Slipping into Lone Eagle's breast plate and leggings, ignoring the squaw's giggling at his nakedness, he had her paint his face with war paint to resemble Lone Eagle himself.

The finishing touch was the long braids he had woven from horse hair. "Lone Eagle!" The old squaw exclaimed, beaming proudly. Now for the Appaloosa stud. Bill wasn't quite sure the stallion was going to let him near him. With his broken leg it would be difficult to control the horse if he spooked from him. Nobody but Lone Eagle himself had ever ridden the great animal. Motioning for Bill to wait, the squaw smeared bear grease in the nostrils of the horse, then cupped her hand around his eye so he couldn't see, as Bill hobbled to where she held him. Kissing the old crone on the cheek, he slapped her on the bottom and eased onto the mighty back. Never had he felt the power in a horse that this one had. If it didn't work Bill knew his leg was going to suffer and his disguise would be in vain.

The stallion stood quiet, waiting for Bill to settle on his broad back. Somehow the stallion sensed the rider needed him to stand. Normally he would have been prancing and raring to go, but this morning with snow covering him, and knowing a new rider was on him, he waited.

The sun was nearly two hours old when the Crows and their allies finally emerged in a long line across the flat that led to the village. A great roar went up from the line of warriors as a huge warrior astride a coal black horse rode out in front of them. Wheeling the horse around in circles he shouted his war cry, and motioned towards the small group of warriors in front of the Sioux lodges. Only silence came from the people as they knew they looked death and destruction in the face. There was just too many of the enemy; they knew the village of High Meadows was doomed.

"There are too many, my Chief." A young warrior looked worried at High Meadows.

Taking a few steps forward, the old Chief held his bow in front of him and towards the enemy. "We are Ogallala Sioux, be brave, have courage, fight for your people."

Suddenly a great shout went up when Bill raced the Appaloosa stud full speed to the center of the flat meadow, halfway towards the Crow, pulling him to a sliding stop.

Throwing down Lone Eagle's war lance he shouted the words the old squaw had taught him, an insult slung in the face of Yellow Moon. Bill knew he had spoken them correctly when a great shout went up behind him.

Bill stepped the stallion a few more feet forward and yelled the insult again, this time turning the horse and showing his backside to the Crow.

"That is not Lone Eagle." Grey Badger spoke, seeing the splint on Bill's leg.

"No, that is my other grandson." Horatio pronounced proudly.

"The Look Alike One is a brave man." Tall Bow spoke from where he stood. "I have another brave son."

"Will he have a chance with a broken leg?" Grey Badger started forward but was stopped by Horatio.

"No, a man only has this chance once in a lifetime. If he lives he will remember this day for the rest of his life."

"And if he dies?" Blue Thunder asked.

"Then my grandson dies with honor and glory, helping his friends the Sioux, who will always remember."

Yellow Moon, sitting his black horse in front of his warriors and savoring the moment before he turned the Crow and Snakes loose on the unprotected village, blinked in disbelief as a warrior raced across the flat and challenged him to fight. His warriors had been lucky, they had caught the warriors of the Sioux away from the village. The victory would be easy, few warriors would be lost.

Now, here sat a warrior on the great Appaloosa war horse. Yes, it was his hated enemy, Lone Eagle. How he had gotten to the village ahead of him Yellow Moon did not know, but there he sat, challenging him to fight. Here was the warrior he hated most of all; now he would have his revenge. Yellow Moon was no coward. He was the greatest warrior of the Crow People, greatly respected by his enemies. Maybe even bigger physically than Lone Eagle; he had no fear. His victories over his enemies had been many. Only this warrior sitting in front of him could be his equal. Today he would kill this one, and his people would see who the greatest warrior was.

Riding the black horse in front of his warriors he extolled them to destroy the village if he failed to kill Lone Eagle. His son and people must be avenged. The two warriors faced each other across a hundred yard span of flat meadow. The spotted stallion started stomping; he could feel the tenseness in Bill's legs and he was eager to run. Bill's blood lust was up, and the yelling of the villagers urging him to victory made his blood race. The great war club of Lone Eagle rested in his hand, light as a feather.

Yellow Moon urged his horse into a run and the great Appaloosa stallion charged forward, his ears laid back, his nostrils flared. The stallion was as courageous as the yelling warrior on his back. Nearer they came, as both horses strained with ever stride. Primitive man took over as the gentleman from Philadelphia reverted back to his ancestors. Not even the great Lone Eagle could feel the taste of combat the way Bill felt it at this moment. The face of death, a mask of ferociousness, made Yellow Moon cringe as he drew near the screaming demon coming straight at him. What was this man, the look of him, screaming like a madman. This one didn't fight for revenge or glory, this one coming on the great spotted stallion fought because he liked to fight.

For the first time in his life Yellow Moon questioned his own invincibility.

25

Virginia and Elizabeth sat their horses watching the village from their vantage point where Lone Eagle had left them as he rode closer to the coming battle. Both women caught their breath as they suddenly realized that it was Lone Eagle sitting the great spotted stallion in the middle of the meadow between the two opposing forces.

"How did he get there so quickly?" Elizabeth asked knowing Lone Eagle had just now left them.

"It is the Look Alike One!" Raven, who had stayed with the women to protect them, spoke.

"Bill!" The name seemed to fall from Elizabeth's stunned mouth.

Lone Eagle was as surprised as everyone else to see himself sitting proud and straight on the Appaloosa stallion, sending forth the fierce war cry of the Ogallala Sioux. When the roar came from the village, Lone Eagle's lips spread into a smile.

"Do well, my brother, for you are truly a brave warrior."

Spread out in a draw alongside the village, Press and the warriors with him could hear the drama unfolding in the meadow above, but could not see what was happening. From Lone Eagle's vantage point he would give the signal to attack, but for now Press would just have to wait blindly. He knew there was something happening in the meadow but couldn't tell what.

"It is the Look Alike One. He has challenged Yellow Moon to fight him," whispered a warrior, hidden on the lip of the gully.

"Bill!" Press scrambled from his horse to where the warrior lay.

"You must wait, Ishta Shakota. To go now would dishonor your brother," The warrior warned.

"His leg!"

"You must wait." Another held Press' arm.

"Yellow Moon is a dead man." The warrior whispered again. "The Look Alike One is an evil spirit."

Close enough to see Bill's face, Press shuddered himself at the look of sheer madness on his friend's face. Sliding back down to the waiting warriors, Press could only shake his head. No, Bill wasn't a demon, but he truly loved a fight. It would take a man like him to defeat the Crow Chief. The two combatants raced forward across the snow covered meadow, the hooves of their horses throwing up large clods of frozen dirt and snow. Both men held their outstretched war clubs menacingly, brandishing them as they neared each other.

From where Press waited he could hear the war clubs banging together like two mountain rams butting their horns together. Fighting on horseback was not new to Bill, as all West Point Cadets were highly trained in cavalry saber techniques. But Yellow Moon himself was an expert too, able to parry Bill's every blow. Both horses were pushing and shoving, sidestepping and circling each other as both men tried to land a fatal blow.

From where he sat, Lone Eagle watched as the struggle continued; two giants unwilling to give an inch. Silently nodding his head, Lone Eagle knew the feelings that each man felt as they fought in this life or death struggle. Watching the face of the Look Alike One, he knew here was one who enjoyed a fight more than even he did. This one was indeed a formidable foe.

Neither man had struck a decisive blow as the battle raged. Yellow Moon dodging a blow from Bill's powerful war club, pulled the head of his horse between himself and Bill. Seeing his opportunity, Bill landed a solid blow to the horse's forehead, causing the horse to crumple under the Appaloosa's hooves.

Flinging himself from the stallion, Bill had to reach the Crow before he could regain his feet. The broken leg would never permit him to move around fast enough to keep away from the Crow's crushing blows. Landing atop Yellow Moon, both men came together, their muscles bulging from the strain as they rolled across the snow packed ground.

The Crow was powerful, Bill thought, as he brought his immense strength to bear upon the man's wrist that held his war club. Grimacing in pain, the Crow held on, straining with all his might. Never had he felt the power like this one had. Like a limb breaking Bill heard the bones in the man's wrist snap and the groan that emitted from his mouth. Wrenching his own wrist loose from the writhing man, he brought his own war club down hard on the man's head killing him instantly. Standing slowly Bill raised his bloody war axe and shouted defiance at the line of Crow warriors. Then to the amazement of the watching warriors, Bill reached down and lifted the dead Crows body above his head, then flung him back to the ground.

With the fall of the great Yellow Moon, the Sioux from the village charged out to meet the oncoming Crow warriors. Undaunted by the loss of their leader, Yellow Moon, the Crows and their Snake allies charged towards the village, unaware of the Sioux warriors on their flanks.

Bill remounted the fractious Appaloosa stallion with great difficulty, as the villagers reached him, and clashed with the enemy. Cutting and slashing his way forward he stopped suddenly as a warrior on a great, gray horse fought his way towards him.

"Well, I wouldn't have believed it." Bill was amazed as he looked upon his twin for the first time. Slapping aside a warrior's war axe he fought his way to Lone Eagle's side.

Each man stared at his own double as their horses came together, then side by side they fought forward. With Sioux warriors in front and on each flank, the Crows fought courageously as they gave ground. Never had they faced warriors who fought with the savagery of Lone Eagle, Bill, and the Sioux.

In the middle of the fight Horatio and High Meadows found themselves surrounded by the enemy. Horatio's slashing saber found its mark time and time again. High Meadows finally went down with an arrow in his back while Horatio fought on, fighting like a man half his age. But the old reflexes failed him just once, allowing a Crow knife to penetrate his side. Slowly the old warrior sank into the blood soaked ground.

Bill, seeing Horatio go down, fought his way through the thickening snow to the old ones side. "Grandfather!"

"Don't worry about me, fight, I'll be alright."

"But?"

"Go, now."

Laying Horatio's head back to the ground, Bill remounted the stallion, and with a reckless look in his eyes rejoined the battle. Songs are still sung around the Sioux campfires about the bravery and ferociousness of the Look Alike One in the Valley of the Dead.

Watching as the Crow and Snake warriors retreated back down the valley, Elizabeth and Virginia quickly urged their horses down towards the village.

Press was holding Horatio as Virginia dismounted and ran to his side. "Grandfather!"

"Don't you fret, Lass I've had worse."

Examining the deep wound, Virginia knew it was no use. Elizabeth held Virginia's medical bag in her hand but dropped it limply when Virginia shook her head.

"Ginny."

"Yes Grandfather."

"My grandsons, bring them to me."

"We are here Grandfather." Bill answered the old man. "Both, of your grandsons."

His eyes trying to focus on the two men who knelt beside him, Horatio smiled and reached for their hands. Holding on to both of them, the old eyes blazed with fire as his lips slowly spread into a smile.

"At last, I have both of you back; now I can rest in peace."

"Don't talk Grandfather." Bill choked back a sob. "Gin!" The dark eyes pleaded for her to do something. Seeing her shoulders shaking Bill looked up into Lone Eagle's face.

Kneeling closer Lone Eagle placed his hand over Horatio's heart and nodded as the General looked up at him. Virginia sobbed uncontrollably as the eyes of the General clouded and slowly closed. "My grandchildren." Were the last words spoken from Andy Jackson's fighting General.

"This was your grandfather." Press spoke quietly to Lone Eagle.

"He was a great warrior. I wish I could have known him better, I am proud to be called his grandson." Lone Eagle folded Horatio's arms across his chest.

Horatio did not die alone that day. High Meadows, his friend, also went to the spirit land. It was indeed a sad day for the Sioux as they lost a great Chief, a good friend, and several of the people. The war drums sounded late into the night as the people celebrated the victory that they had won, and at the same time mourned their losses.

26

Horatio was buried beside High Meadows, one in a grave, the white man's way, the other on a scaffold, the Lakota way, so his spirit could soar with the eagles on his way to the next world. Both men were buried with honors; the General and High Meadows were both great leaders and protectors of their people, deserving the greatest respect that could be given them.

As soon as the burials were finished, the village moved on to where the buffalo had been located. Necessity made it impossible to mourn for High Meadows as long as was traditional. The buffalo had been found and without meat and hides the people would perish in the oncoming winter months ahead. The high, cold, north country, had no sympathy on the weak nor the ones ill prepared to meet the harsh winds and heavy snows that were coming.

The village passed by the tall scaffold and the small mound of dirt. All eyes looked, but the horses plodded on, not stopping, pulling the travois and carrying the teary eyed ones away from the Valley of the Dead. No longer would this place be the summer camping grounds of the people. Too many bad reminders of the terrible fight would forever remind them of their loved ones.

The second day found the village again spread out along a flat valley. The great herd was only a short distance away. Press and Bill were mounted, ready to ride with the warriors. Lone Eagle was again mounted on his favorite Appaloosa stallion. Bill had been presented the black horse of Yellow Moon, and was astride him. Tall Bow was beaming and proud of the gray stallion Lone Eagle had given him.

"If only Wild Horse was here." Tall Bow looked to the north.

"He will be here soon, my father." Lone Eagle smiled. After the battle, Grey Badger had ridden out to find Wild Horse, and had returned with the good news that Wild Horse was coming along slowly behind him.

Lone Eagle had wanted to go bring him in, but Tall Bow, who was now Chief of the Ogalallas taking the place of his brother High Meadows, had advised that all the warriors were needed to keep the village safe while the buffalo were being hunted.

As the scouts motioned the hunters forward, Press looked to where Bill sat the black. "Leg alright, you strong enough to ride?"

Patting the neck of the prancing horse, Bill grinned. "Just don't you and that scrawny runt you're riding get lost."

Press nodded his head. For once Bill was right, compared to the black his sorrel was small, but the horse and rider had come a long way across these prairies together. The sorrel had a great heart and the speed to stay up.

"We'll do our best."

"See you on the other side then." Bill reached across and slapped Press on the back.

The earth trembled as the frightened herd ran from the screaming devils that pursued them. The dust and flying dirt drifting above the laboring buffalo obliterated everything, except the closest of the fleeing animals. Arrows, spears, and gunfire, added to the pandemonium that broke out as the riders on the fast buffalo runners descended into the midst of the great herd.

Miles faded behind him as Press fired, reloaded and fired again. Finally, as the herd disintegrated into small bunches, and the sorrel was completely winded from the chase, Press pulled him to a stop. Dead buffalo dotted the horizon for miles. Turning the sorrel, Press rode back to find Bill sitting tiredly on a dead buffalo carcass.

"I've never imagined such a thing." Bill was tired, but his face was elated.

"The village will have all the meat they'll need this winter." Press agreed, looking up to see the whole village converging to start skinning and packing the meat back to the village for hanging and curing. Lone Eagle rode up and slid easily from the spotted stallion's back. A red film of dirt covered his huge chest.

"We have killed many."

Press and Bill both nodded. Indeed the kill had been mightier than any known before. No empty stomachs would be found in the lodges of the Sioux people during the hungry times ahead.

"You will winter with us this year, my brothers."

"No, I must return to run our business before it falls dead like these buffalo." Bill motioned to the dead buffalo, trying to make his words so Lone Eagle could understand.

"What is business?" Lone Eagle did not understand.

Press helped as Bill's Sioux was still not very understandable. "He means like your horse herds, they could run away if he is not there to watch them."

"If horses run away we'll steal more. The Crows do not mind." Lone Eagle laughed. "Ishta Shakota is a good horse stealer."

"Oh, no!" Press laughed and raised his arms. "My horse raiding days are over."

"With a little help, you'll make a good horse stealer."

"No, my brother; I must rejoin the people at the fort before they throw me in the iron cage. But the Medicine Woman and I will come back soon."

"Tell me again, what is business?" Lone Eagle was curious.

"My brother, Lone Eagle is a very rich man." Bill tried to explain.

"Rich?"

"Yes, that means you can have anything you want." Press explained.

"I already have everything I want, except one thing." Lone Eagle looked to where Virginia and Elizabeth were approaching.

A worried look came across Press' face as he looked to where Lone Eagle gazed, then back at Bill. "The lady has already promised herself to me, my brother, but I do not object to you trying your luck." Press explained Bill's words to Lone Eagle.

Lone Eagle studied Bill's face then looked over to where Press sat. "That is good; do not worry, I have given Ishta Shakota my word. There will be no trouble the woman will go with the one she chooses."

"Did he say he gave his word?" Bill was curious.

"Something like that, nothing really." Press lied.

Virginia and Elizabeth rode to where the three men sat. Amazed at the amount of buffalo killed, the women started trying to count the carcasses lying in view.

"You three are sure serious." Virginia spoke, finally giving up on her counting. Elizabeth now, being the bookkeeper she was, kept at it until Press' words finally dawned on her.

"And Mr. Forbes, would you mind explaining what you meant, that they are deciding who gets me?" Elizabeth stared hard at the men.

Press started figuring a way to try and explain his way out of this predicament when a shout went up from the people. Looking behind them they saw a group of warriors surrounding Wild Horse. With a howl of joy Lone Eagle raced to his brother.

"Well Mr. Forbes, I'm waiting." Elizabeth looked questionly at Press.

"Yes ma'am, you are, but I've got to see a man." Press loped his horse after Lone Eagle, leaving Bill and the women laughing behind.

Everyone was laughing and talking at once as Press stopped alongside Lone Eagle. Studying the laughing young warrior, Press could tell instantly why everybody loved him. Sometimes a persons charm comes through so strong you're captivated by them. And this was Wild Horse, unpredictable, wild, but the people loved him. Especially Lone Eagle, Press could tell the warrior doted on his younger brother.

"My brother." Lone Eagle looked to where Bill had ridden up beside Press. "These are your brothers. The Look Alike One and Ishta Shakota."

Press watched the expression on Wild Horse' face as he looked at Bill, then back to Lone Eagle. "The Great Spirit plays a joke on me. Now I have two ugly brothers that look the same. And you Ishta Shakota, I have heard much of your bravery."

Wild Horse rode up between Press and Bill and put both of his arms out to them. Virginia, Elizabeth, and Raven had followed Bill to the gathering of the warriors. Shaking hands, Wild Horse kneed his gelding on forward to where the women waited.

Virginia smiled and reached out her hands. "You are stronger. How is your wound?"

Press translated for her and for once Wild Horse was serious. "I feel good, and the Crow women did not get to put me on their fire. Yes Medicine Woman, you have given me my life Back; and now, I have a sister too. I am fortunate. And I thank you too." Wild Horse smiled at Elizabeth.

A week passed and meat hung on racks throughout the village. Hides were pegged everywhere throughout the lodges. Yes, this year would indeed be a time of plenty for the people. True to his word, Bill had not interfered with Lone Eagle's courtship of Elizabeth. She was never alone, either Lone Eagle or Bill was in her company. Bill had taken the young Wild Horse under his wing, teaching him of the white man's rifle and many of their ways. Bill, much to Press' amazement, genuinely liked the young warrior, going so far as to try and convince Wild Horse to accompany him back east.

"Who are our enemies in the east?" Wild Horse asked.

"We don't have enemies; not fighting enemies."

"No horse stealing, no women, no scalps?"

"No."

Wild Horse shook his head and grinned. "Thank you, my brother, but Wild Horse will stay here."

"Well, maybe one day you will come and see the marvels of the white man."

"One day, perhaps." Wild Horse was dubious.

Bill's leg was almost mended. He would always have a slight limp, but he was walking. He was ready to head east before the heavy snows made it impossible to travel. No slow moving wagons or oxen this time, only fast horses. Raven and Crow Foot along with a few warriors from the village would see them safely to Lame Bull's village, then they to would return too their people. Bill was eager and ready to go. He was ready. Philadelphia called.

"Ah Gin, it's going to be good to get home, isn't it?" Bill laughed leaning down to look in Virginia's eyes.

"I won't be going to Philadelphia."

"What?"

"Press and I will be married when we get back to the fort."

"Great, then both of you can come east with me and Elizabeth."

"No Bill, Press is going to resign from the army, and open his own trading post."

"You're not serious!" Bill was incredulous.

"Yes, very serious."

Bill was concentrating so hard on what his sister had just said he was unaware of Press walking up. "You two are staying out here when I need you to help run Grandfather's business?"

Virginia hooked her arm in Bill's and squeezed him. "You don't need us. You are twice the businessman Press is."

"I do need you."

"No Bill, you've got Elizabeth now, do we have your blessings?"

Bill noticed Press for the first time. "Does it matter?"

"Yes, very much."

"Then you have my blessings." Bill smiled, shaking hands with Press and hugging Virginia. "But remember Preston keep a water trough close at hand."

"That'll be enough of that, William Lane." Virginia laughed.

Press and Virginia watched as Bill walked back through the village towards his lodge. Elizabeth was not in sight. The sun was setting and the skies were darkening. The heavy snows were not far off.

"We need to start back tomorrow."

"Do you think Elizabeth will be going with us?" Virginia asked.

"I don't know, neither does Bill." Press frowned. "That's why he has delayed so long."

"I think it's just now that he really knows he needs her, and that he loves her."

"I think you're right." Press agreed. "Anyway he has been a man and has given her time to be sure."

"With Elizabeth, I wonder if there is ever enough time." Virginia laughed.

The temperature started dropping with the setting of the sun, so everyone retreated to Bill and Press' lodge. Buffalo steaks and wild onions were simmering across the fire when Lone Eagle and Elizabeth stooped through the entrance. The carefree atmosphere in the lodge diminished when Press made the announcement of their intended departure early in the morning.

"Leaving, in the morning, so soon?" Elizabeth looked to where Virginia set.

"It is time to leave, the snows are coming and Grandfather's business needs us."

"Us?" Elizabeth stammered.

"We are a team, are we not?"

"Bill, let's go for a walk." Elizabeth took his arm leading him outside.

Virginia shook her head. Whatever happened tomorrow one of her brothers would be sadder. Moving closer to Lone Eagle, he was surprised when she leaned against his broad shoulder. Neither spoke as they looked into the fire. Tall Bow and Wild Horse nodded, then trying to lighten the moment, dug into the simmering meat.

The village was on the move, headed for their protected valley that would keep out the harsh winter winds. The people had passed smiling and waving goodbye as the small party headed east. Tall Bow and Wild Horse sat their horses then both men gripped the arms of Press and Bill.

Wild Horse wrapped a beautiful sewed fox coat around Virginia's shoulders. "When my sister wears this she will be warm."

"Thank you, my brother." Virginia leaned from her horse and kissed the blushing Wild Horse.

With a wave of his hand Tall Bow loped to the head of the column without looking back. Only Lone Eagle and Wild Horse remained. Virginia rode near Lone Eagle and held his hand.

Virginia looked at Press and smiled. "Tell my brother, I am glad we have finally found each other, my heart will be sad until we meet again." Press interpreted her words.

"In the spring we will come to the fort to see our sister and Ishta Shakota." Lone Eagle smiled down at her.

"Ishta Shakota will take good care of my sister?"

"Yes, Wild Horse, I will take very good care of her." Press nodded at the youngster.

"That is good. Your scalp would not look good over my fire." Wild Horse laughed and kicked his horse into a hard run, yelling his war cry.

Bill and Lone Eagle locked arms, both so identical in looks but so very, very different. "Goodbye, my brother."

"Goodbye, Phillip."

"Will you come back to the people so we can hunt the buffalo again?" Lone Eagle asked solemnly.

"I will return one day."

"Good, the Ogalalla will be waiting."

The warriors that were to escort the small party back to the fort turned their horses and set off to the east, leaving only Lone Eagle and Elizabeth behind. Bill did not look back, just rode, his eyes boring into the warrior's back in front of him. Elizabeth rode close to Lone Eagle, her knee touching his, her eyes studying and remembering every inch of his strong face.

"I must go with him, he needs me." She sobbed, tears running down her face. She knew he could not understand her words. "Goodbye, my love." Elizabeth kissed the big warrior then with a slap of her riding quirt raced to catch up with Bill.

Lone Eagle sat the big Appaloosa stallion and watched her ride off. Lifting his massive arm he waved as she reined in beside Bill. Bill looked at her as she dabbed a hand to her eyes. Turning in his saddle he looked to where Lone Eagle still sat the stallion. Studying his huge hands he looked again at Elizabeth.

"Miss Hudson."

"Yes, Mr. Lane." Elizabeth tried to smile at him.

"As I am now in total control of Lane Enterprises, your services will no longer be needed."

"What?" Elizabeth stammered. "What are you saying?"

"I'm saying, my dear, you are dismissed, fired, no longer working for me." Bill tried his best to be gruff, knowing it hadn't worked. "Do you understand?"

"Oh yes, yes."

Turning the Appaloosa stallion back towards the moving village, Lone Eagle looked back one last time as Elizabeth kissed Bill then averted his eyes. Seconds later hearing the hoof beats of a hard running horse, he turned and smiled as Elizabeth pulled her horse up next to him. Reaching out she took his hand in hers. Stopping their horses, the great Sioux warrior Lone Eagle and the Philadelphia Belle sat and watched as the small party slowly disappeared into the drifting snow.

The End

978-0-595-49145-2
0-595-49145-6